MW00584174

Help Me Hold Onto This

Help Me Hold Onto This

Zachary Leonard

Published by Tablo

Table of Contents

Dedication   1

Foreword by Tyler Blanton   3

Wait, What?   5

Whatever All Of This Is   17

Dating App   25

Hope Is A Heartache   35

L   55

I   67

A   77

R   91

Mess Me Up   97

I Hope You Think Of Me   113

How To Measure Infinity   127

Last October Fifth   141

That's Not What I Meant   147

Help Me Hold Onto You   155

For my parents and my siblings, and for all of the characters in my life that have inspired these stories.

Foreword by Tyler Blanton

When I met Zachary Leonard, it was through a mutual friend.
At the time our friend worked for a since-closed pie shop in
Denver, Colorado and it was at the bar there that we were first
acquainted. I remember him hard at work typing on his laptop,
a beer set in front of him, doing the familiar mental gymnastics
that come with writing. I had come in to chat and luckily he
welcomed a distraction in the form of my company, and I will
always be grateful that he did. Almost immediately, it was
clear to me that he was a storyteller. I remember sipping
whiskey, my eyes wide open, in awe of some of the stories he
told of his travels and his everyday life. Highlighting the chaos
that can arise from the mundane and excitement of
experiencing new places, he was the personification, for me, of
what it meant to live a well-traveled, dramatic life, always
prepared to keep on moving through hard times and never
afraid to share.

A few years have passed now since that meeting, and I have
come to hear so many more of Zachary's stories, both real and
imagined, and cannot say how much of a pleasure it is to
introduce this collection of them to you. I have heard what
drives the ideas, discussed ways to develop them further, read
drafts, and have been fortunate enough to be present for some
of the events that inspired them. I can say, too, that this
experience has truly helped me grow. Zachary's words have
given me an enhanced understanding of the depths that lie
behind the tiny gestures and the nuances of our lives when

they involve people that we love. We each, I believe, have a set of tiny somethings that mean the world to us, and you would be hard-pressed, reader, to finish this book without relating to it.

To put into words the little victories and the little deaths that make up characters with intimate, fulfilling, and, at times, troubled personal lives requires not only a deft craftsman but also an emotionally generous mind. Fiction, at its best, is here to take us through the experience of being someone else and then leave us feeling more connected to our worlds. With this volume, that is exactly what you can expect. These stories will place you behind the eyes of their characters and guide you through stories that underline the significance of moments both large and small, both good and bad. Whether from a gentle kiss on the forehead, an unexpected display of affection, an unwelcome diagnosis, or the process of learning to trust, it is through these stories I have come to understand that every aspect of our lives, every blip on the radar, is so much more meaningful than we may initially realize.

When you flip through these next few pages and dive into the experiences and imaginings of my dearest friend, I ask that you keep both your mind and your heart open. Since the first day I met Zachary, I knew I had to do the same that I ask of you, and he has only ever led me to a better understanding of him, of myself, and of the world around me. And truly, reader, when we sit down to enjoy fiction, isn't that the point?

Wait, What?

I was not drunk, just slightly inebriated. I'm pretty sure of that. I didn't love to drink but I needed it in social situations like this one. Otherwise, I'd have been sitting in the corner sipping my soda water in silence. Instead, I had two vodka sodas and three shots of tequila.

We were celebrating my friend Becca being published in a big magazine for the first time.

Maybe I was drunk, because there I was stumbling over to some hot guy in a flannel shirt at this gay bar, a place I'd normally never go, keeping hard eye contact to let him know that it was him I was coming towards.

"HEY," I said, or maybe I shouted it.

"Hi," he replied without even looking my way.

"Oh, uh, oh god I didn't think this through."

"What?" he asked turning my way. "I can't hear you, the music is so loud."

"I really like your hairline," I said, and he shifted uncomfortably. "I mean, um, you have really great hair. My hair has been falling out since I was sixteen so I really appreciate a, uh, good hairline."

He smiled politely and said he needed to use the restroom. I turned and walked back towards Becca, who had sent me his way.

"Awe how'd it go?" She asked.

"Not well," I said to her then asked the bartender for another shot of tequila. "How is it that I literally do not know how to talk to people? I can't even have a simple conversation without making a fool of myself." I tilted the shot into my mouth and bit the lime.

"I think I have to kill him," I said with a gulp to get rid of the bad taste.

"Ummm, what?"

"I literally just complimented that beautiful man on his hairline. I have to kill him before he tells everyone how pathetic I am."

"Ohhh shut up," Becca said and ordered me another shot of tequila.

"I have to flirt with someone else tonight," I said after I threw back the shot. "I have to redeem myself from that embarrassment somehow."

"Well let's look around and see who we can find for you!"

"No. That's too much work. I'll just text David."

My head spun as I pulled my phone out of my pocket and struggled to make different facial expressions to unlock the device. Becca tried to grab the phone from my hands but I pulled back before she could get it.

"You are not texting David! Or any of your exes for that matter!"

"Awe," I had hit the wall of intoxication. One would definitely consider me a mess. "Come on, I only have like two - wait three- exes. No biggie."

When I woke the next morning, my head was pounding and the sun was screaming. I sat up and looked around the room that wasn't mine. Blank white walls, green plants, a desk with a notepad, and a blue and purple flannel shirt hanging on the back of the door.

My phone started vibrating in my pocket. I was half thankful I didn't lose my phone and half thankful that I was still wearing all of my clothes. It was Becca calling.

"Hello?" I said softly so that I didn't make my presence known to whomever the apartment belonged.

"Hey, where are you? I have called you like a hundred times. I have been so worried!"

"I'm okay, I'm okay," I said to calm her down. "I honestly don't know where I am. I must have gone home with someone last night."

I was embarrassed to admit it. Going home with strangers wasn't something I did. I was by no means a prude, but let's be honest, I was definitely a prude.

"Oh," her tone changed from worry to a flirtatious excitement. "And how did that go?"

"Uh, I have no idea. I can't remember anything. I just woke up in this bed alone a minute ago. My head is killing me."

"Oh my what are you going to do?" I could hear footsteps coming from outside the door.

"I'm not sure yet but I have to go," I said and hung up.

The doorknob spun and the door opened slowly as if whoever was on the other side knew I might still be sleeping and didn't want to wake me. I sat there frozen in shock when the guy on the other side of the door was revealed. Now I remember why the flannel was so familiar. It was hairline guy.

"Hey stud," the words flew from his mouth so casually. He was in nothing but boxers and was carrying two coffee cups, one green, and one purple. "I hope you like hazelnut. It's the only creamer flavor I like."

I was stuck, unable to answer because of two reasons: 1) I also can only drink coffee if I have hazelnut creamer, and 2) abs.

He walked towards the bed and extended the purple cup in my direction. I took the it in my hands and considered what to say next. Carefully, as to not spill his own drink, he climbed up onto the bed and sat down beside me.

"I'm Harrison," he said. I introduced myself and thanked him for the coffee.

"Hazelnut is my favorite too," I said and he smiled. "I have to be honest I am not completely sure how I got here."

"That's okay," he said before taking a long sip of his coffee. "You were pretty drunk. Don't worry though, we didn't have sex or anything. Just cuddled some."

Somehow after years of being single and going on horrible dates, I had accidentally fallen into the bed of a man that I would never normally even look at twice for fear of being rejected.

"Oh well, that's good to hear," I said almost sarcastically. "I mean, not that I don't find you attractive. I'm just happy we didn't have sex because...well, actually," I stopped and thought about what to say next before my brain melted and I made a complete fool of myself. All I could come up with was, "You make me really nervous."

He smiled and said, "I can tell. It's okay. Maybe I should have made you decaf?" I smiled and took a sip of the hazelnut flavored coffee.

"So," I started hesitantly. "What are your plans for the day?" He set his coffee down on the nightstand. The way he moved so effortlessly, so confidently, so much better than me.

"I have some errands to run today, some shopping to do," he got up and pulled a plain grey t-shirt over his head and onto his body. "But I am free tonight if you want to grab a drink? Or dinner maybe?"

I had to stop and think about it, and when he saw my eyes

widen in surprise he giggled. How did I end up in this situation? This was the guy who last night could barely look me in the eyes, and now I am somehow in his bed, and even further, he wants to spend more time with me?

"How about I give you my number and you can let me know?"

"Sure, that sounds good," I said hating myself for not being better at this. He walked over to where the flannel he was wearing the night before hung, pulled it down, and threw it towards me.

"Put that on and I'll drive you home," He said. "It's cold this morning and you only have that t-shirt on."

Later that day I met Becca at our go-to coffee shop. The cafe was actually called "Coffee Shop" and we loved it because of the good music and the even better mochas.

Becca was eager to hear everything. When Harrison dropped me off at my apartment, I had just enough time to change clothes and brush my teeth before she pulled up to go get coffee.

"Nice shirt," she said as I climbed into the passenger seat of her car. "That looks familiar." She was smiling because she knew exactly where the cold colored flannel came from.

After we got our coffee, we sat at our normal spot. I told her everything that happened, and since there wasn't much, we quickly moved on to silently working on our own projects. I sat with my laptop, her with a notepad and pencil.

I had my second cup of coffee and I was finally settled in to get some work done when I felt a tap on my shoulder.

"Mind if I join you?" A voice asked from behind me. I looked up at Becca who was smiling wide-eyed and then I turned around to see Harrison standing there. He was wearing a baseball cap and my god he looked so good.

"Oh! Hi!" I was stunned. The last person I thought I would see here still looking like a mess from the night before, still wearing his shirt. My cheeks were hot and, of course, I knocked over my coffee.

"What're you doing here?" I asked as he pulled me in for a hug. I could feel Becca's excited eyes on me. "I thought you had some errands to run today?"

"It turns out one of my errands involves working on my laptop with a good cup of coffee." He smiled and my world fell apart.

What was happening to me? Of course, I had never been the most confident person but normally I was not such a bumbling idiot. I apologized to the barista who was tasked to clean the coffee mess I made on the floor, while Becca introduced herself to Harrison and told him to take her seat, that she was headed out.

"Wait..?" I asked. "You're leaving?"

"Yeah," Becca said. "I have to go home and get ready for work, but I have a feeling you aren't going to be too lonely."

She was lying. Saturdays were Becca's one day off from her serving job. I thought about challenging her, but decided I should take the opportunity to see what Harrison was really looking to get from me. I gave Becca a hug and a smirk and she was on her way.

Harrison and I sat across from each other, both our laptops open. The barista brought me a new cup of coffee and I apologized again.

"So what are you working on?" Harrison asked. I was hesitant on how honest I should be with him. Being a full-time writer is tough to explain, because people either have zero respect for the craft, or they have an obscure idea of what a writer actually does. I decided to give him the benefit of the doubt.

"I'm a writer. I'm writing a book."

"Really!" He said, obviously impressed.

"Yeah, it's been my life for a couple of years now. What do you do for work?"

"I work in advertising. It's okay but not at all as interesting as being a writer," he said with a side eye smirk. "Can I ask you what the book is about?"

My muscles were starting to relax. I could feel myself growing more comfortable with this person. There was something so welcoming about him, so genuine, so gracious. Nothing like the men I normally met. Which why I was slightly embarrassed to respond with, "It's a series of short stories about some of my horrible experiences with the gay community."

A point in the conversation where people normally backed up, Harrison leaned in, and that was it. All at once I felt a rush in my body that was giving myself over to him. I was skeptical until then, but now I knew it: I had a crush, and I hoped he had one on me too.

"So is it a memoir then?"

"Well, I have definitely pulled a lot of small details from personal experience, but I have fictionalized it enough that I wouldn't call any of it actually true."

"Very interesting," he took a sip of his coffee. "I can't wait to read it. I'm legitimately intrigued."

"Well who knows, maybe you'll end up inspiring a story."

We both laughed.

That evening I changed my shirt six times before settling into a plain grey shirt with a navy blue cardigan and blue jeans. Not casual but not too fancy either. I wanted to look nice but not like I was trying too hard even though, obviously, I was.

After an hour of small talk in the coffee shop, Harrison had to go but asked me if I would wanna meet him for a drink that night. I confidently said yes. I wanted to know him better. Know him more than just a night of drunken cuddling and an hour at a coffee shop discussing our favorite colors and bands.

I combed my hair and brushed my teeth for three minutes instead of the recommended two. Extra deodorant, just in case, and I filed my nails down so I couldn't even try to bite them if I felt anxious.

Our plan was he would pick me up at five but I was standing ready at the front door of my apartment complex at ten till. I wanted to make an impression. I didn't want to keep him waiting. I wanted him to see that this was important to me. That, maybe, with the right chemistry, he could be important to me.

When he pulled up I skipped down the steps that lead to the street. In a moment that would usually give me anxiety, I felt calm and collected and ready.

"Hey there," he said as I climbed into his car and pulled the door shut.

"Hi," I said with a smile.

"Are you hungry?" He asked. "I know a great Mexican place."

"That sounds great!" I said.

We drove to the other side of town where the restaurant was and took turns playing our favorite songs and talking about how the rest of our days went. His work meeting that ran too long causing him to almost be late picking me up. My complete writers' block after he left me at the coffee shop. We told stories and laughed and happiness fell into place.

We sat across from each other at the restaurant, margaritas in hand. "So," Harrison said after we clinked our glasses. "What do I need to know about you? What's something people don't know about you?"

"Hmm," I thought. "Well as a writer, I am pretty much an open book. You can ask me whatever you'd like."

He sat back in his chair quizzically, "Do you have siblings?" He asked.

"Yes, two older sisters and one older brother."

"And you're out to them?"

"Of course. My whole family knows."

He smiled and nodded. Like I had passed a test. "And how is your relationship with your parents?"

"It's...complicated," I said. "But getting better every day."

"That's so wonderful!"

"Yeah," I said with a nod. "It was mostly me and my mom. It feels like I am at the end of a hard race with her. Like we were taking turns being in first place and finally, we figured out that we could cross the finish line together."

"Hmm," he leaned forward in his chair. "Do you ever write about her?"

"I do, but I would never publish anything that is so blatantly about the stuff we have gone through. It was a lot of miscommunication and I could probably write an entire series of it but I love her, and I don't want to hurt her by publishing something too incredibly honest when mostly there was just a lot of confusion between us. Neither of us were ever at fault I don't believe."

He smiled, "That's good. Moms are important, and dads too."

"I agree," I replied. "It's weird I never talk about it. I'm usually too shy to let it be brought up."

"It can be tough sometimes for sure."

"How is your relationship with your parents? Any siblings?"

"I actually don't have any siblings and my parents passed away a few years ago."

"Oh, I'm so sorry, I didn't…"

"It's okay," he assured me with a subtle smile.

The server dropped off two plates of tacos in front of us and refilled our basket of chips. I wasn't exactly sure how to move the conversation forward, so I was happy when, finally, he said, "Yeah, it was a tough few years but I had good people in my life to take care of me."

I envied him. I had plenty of friends, but being a writer was sporadic just enough that it was tough to keep relationships alive. Late nights with a bottle of wine on the balcony of my apartment, early mornings in coffee shops beating my head on the table when my brain refused to function.

Of course, I had Becca, but she was also a writer and a lot of times our schedules didn't align properly. And when they did, our moods didn't. I needed loud when she needed quiet. She needed wine when I need espresso.

"I am happy you have good people," I said. "Sometimes I feel like I don't have that. Like if something bad happened to my parents or siblings, I wouldn't have anyone or anything to fall on but my career"

"I think people will surprise you with how much they actually care. I think people will surprise you in general."

"You're right," I said thinking about how, even after only knowing him for a day and a half, I'd drop everything for Harrison if he needed me.

"How about after this we go over to this bar I know." He

said and gulped down the rest of his margarita. I followed suit. "I have a few friends I want you to meet."

We drove back across town with the windows down. When he was focused on the roads I'd look his way and imagined what this could possibly end up being. Was I really the one to attract such a beautifully charismatic man into my life. And now he wanted me to meet his friends. I don't even remember the last time a boy I was talking to introduced me to his friends.

I spent the past three years of my life single and holding myself up and together and doing everything I could to avoid stomach butterflies and get love quick schemes. And eventually, I felt nothing about anyone ever. There wasn't a single guy that I met that made me stutter and trip on my feelings, until this guy right here, who was unbelievably gorgeous and was actually smart and kind.

We got to the bar and he pulled me by my left hand through a crowd of people lit up with different colored stage lights. The music was live but not too loud that you couldn't have a conversation.

He pulled me through to a back corner where a group of his friends were sitting at a table. He let go of my hand to hug his friends, one by one.

The last guy he hugged was tall and thin, with long hair pulled back into a messy bun. He pulled him over to where I was to introduce us.

"I'd like you to meet my boyfriend, Jonathan," he said and the boy reached his hand out to shake mine.

"Hey, it's great to meet ya!" He said. "Harrison was telling me about your drunken night together...so funny!"

"I...wait, what?"

Whatever All Of This Is

"You have gonorrhea," the doctor said plainly. Like he was telling me I had the common cold. Like it was no big deal. I honestly couldn't help but laugh a little bit. Or a lot. And soon, he stood there in silence while I full on cackled.

The sounds of my laughter bounced around the sterile white room of the clinic. The paper I was sitting on crunched and the doctor, with his glasses low on his nose, stared at me.

"Are you okay?" he asked me. I'm sure he thought I was insane. That the sexually transmitted infection had reached my brain and was making me mad.

"Yeah, I'm okay," I said calming myself down. "It's just funny."

"How so?" he asked and I started giggling again.

"Because I am the biggest prude you'll probably ever meet. I don't have sex for this exact reason! Because I am so terrified of something like this happening. And last month I was home alone and feeling a certain way, if you know what I mean," I started to choke on my words. "And so I texted my ex-boyfriend. I picked him up in the middle of the night and we had sex in the back seat of my car in the middle of a Taco Bell parking lot."

It felt good to get it out but now I was crying. Hysterically crying while this old doctor stared at me probably terrified of the mess that was unfolding in front of him.

"And he gave me fucking gonorrhea. I mean how random is that? The boy I was happily in love with and who broke my heart has gonorrhea and he gave it to me! I don't know whose karma this is, his or mine, but it's funny and sad and..." I had more to say but I was crying too hard to get it out.

"Right," the doctor interjected. "Well, the treatment is really very easy. A nurse will be in soon to administer the shot to you and you'll have ten days' worth of antibiotics. And really, I hope you get past," he moved his hand in a circle gesturing at all of me, "whatever all of this is." And then he left.

A few days later and my symptoms were almost completely gone. I laid in bed on my day off, still unsure of how to tell David about it. Should I call him? Was a "Hey, you gave me gonorrhea" text good enough? Was it proper etiquette? I wasn't sure what to do in this situation that I never thought I'd find myself in.

What if he knew and had already been to a doctor and wasn't planning on telling me? Or what if he thought it was me that gave it to him?

Most likely, he didn't know he had it at all. I knew very little about sexually transmitted infections, but what I do remember from that terribly awkward day of sexual education in middle school is that different people may have different symptoms, or maybe none at all.

My biggest fear was that he would tell me I must've gotten it somewhere else; that I probably was the one that gave it to him even though we both know that's not true. Even he would know that whether he wanted to believe it or not. I am too emotional for random hook-ups with random strangers, and he knows it.

I sent him a text: *Think you could stop by my apartment today?*

He responded: *I have to work in a few hours, but I'm free now.*

And within ten minutes I was buzzing him into the apartment complex. Not enough time to decide exactly how to tell him, but I guessed I would have to play it by ear.

A knock on the door. A flail in my chest. How could I possibly tell him this? I opened the door and David embraced me. He slammed the door behind him, spun us both around, shoved me back up against it, and started to kiss me.

It felt good to be wanted like this by him again. I pulled his jacket off of him and his shirt next and my hands roamed his whole body before I remembered this isn't why I invited him over today. This was actually the worst thing that could happen.

"David, we ca-" I tried to get out but he interrupted my words with more kisses. He moved to my neck and I said, "David we can't be doing this."

"Why not?" he said into my neck. "Why are we doing this to ourselves? I miss you. I want to be with you." He tugged at my shirt and I let him pull it off of me.

He was saying everything I wanted to hear. Everything I wanted to say. Why were we doing this? Why were we torturing ourselves by being apart.

"David, we just can't do this right *now,*" I said as firmly as I could muster, even though he was on the sensitive spot where my neck merged with my chest at my collar bone.

"It sure seems like you're enjoying yourself," he said as he moved down further.

"I have gonorrhea," I let out like a hiccup, and he stopped with his face frozen at my belt line.

Slowly, he got up from his knees so we were face to face.

"How long have you known?" He asked.

"A few days," I said. "I got tested and treated and I'll be

okay by the end of the week."

I saw his eyes doing the math in his head. From the time when we were still together to when we broke up. From when he slept with someone else and contracted the infection to the night when he passed it on to me.

"I knew I had it," he said as he left me and went and sat down on the couch. His face in his hands.

"You knew?" I said. Any sympathy I had was gone, and honestly, I think I could have punched him in the dick for it.

"Yes, I knew but I thought it would be gone by the time I was with you again. I was tested and got the shot and that was at least ten days before we slept together. Anything less and I never would have considered it."

The ticking of the clock on my living room wall seemed louder than normal. The only noise to put a break between my emotions and his. But honestly, I had no idea what I felt. Somewhere stuck between anger and understanding. I sat down next to him on the couch and put my arm around him.

"It's okay," I said. "I know you wouldn't do anything to purposely hurt me." He pulled his face from his hands and leaned into me, and I added, "But also, we both need to get our shit together."

He nodded into my chest. We sat there cuddled on the couch, our arms and legs tangled. I tried to think of the last time I felt this good with David. And was there something wrong if it was a sexually transmitted infection that brought us back together?

"Did you really think I called you for a quickie?" I asked remembering how fast he jumped me when coming through the front door. David sat up and looked at me nervously. "It's okay if that's what you thought, but where does that leave us?"

He looked around the newly green room. "You painted,"

he said, avoiding the question, which of course was an answer in itself.

"Yeah, it's been a weird couple of months."

"What was wrong with the blue?"

"It felt too sad. I was sad, and the room felt sad. And green felt," I stopped to think of the right word. "I don't know. Fresh? Like the beginning and not the end of something."

The room not only had a new color but was also rearranged and messier than normal. Sheets of work papers scattered heavily across the desk, a candle burnt passed its expiration, unfolded blankets on the floor around the couch.

"I'm sorry I gave you gonorrhea," David said shyly putting his head back into my chest.

"I forgive you," I said even though I wasn't sure if I actually had.

The next morning I laid in my bed, uncomfortable. My entire body felt off. Like the meds that were working against the infection in my body were attacking the wrong cells. How could he do this to me? How could I do this to myself?

I was ready to take part of the blame. After all, we should not have been hooking up. I should not have called him that night like I did. We weren't together at that point, and he had every right to sleep with whomever he wanted.

But still, it made me question every part of our relationship. If it was so easy for him to have a random hook up now, who knew how easy it could have been for him at any time. Especially during our final year of college when we lived a full three hours away from each other.

My phone vibrated on the nightstand. I unlocked the device to see a text from my friend Becca asking to meet her for a drink.

"I am on antibiotics for a few more days so I can't drink but sure I'll meet ya," I responded.

"Why? Are you sick?" She texted back.

"I'll catch you up when I see you," I added a crying laughing emoji and hit send.

A week passed and I felt completely normal again. No more symptoms, no more gonorrhea. Which meant one thing: David and I could talk about what was next for us.

We decided to meet at a coffee shop we frequented when we were still officially together. The barista knew us by name and gave us free coffee when his manager wasn't around. David always argued that it was because he thought I was cute and I argued that maybe he was just a nice guy to all of the frequent coffee shop patrons.

I sat alone on the couch in the back, reading a book that a co-worker gifted me at our last holiday party. A murder mystery book wasn't my normal go-to but I decided I would read it to be polite. So I could act shocked about how the person you least expected ended up being the killer even though it was foreshadowed on the very first page.

The book was actually holding my attention until I heard David's voice saying hello to Eddie, the barista with the free coffee. I watched as he talked and chastised myself for ever letting that beautiful man get away from me in the first place.

How could three years end in a single moment? Because of what? I was in a bad mood that day? Or because his anxiety kept him up late the night before? There wasn't a real reason for it. It was like a tornado touching down. A fight that only lasted a couple of minutes but the damage would take months to fix

"Hey," he said as he took a seat next to me with his iced mocha.

"Good morning," I said with a smile, folding the edge of the book page to keep my place. David had obviously tried to make himself look extra nice. His hair had gel in it, he was wearing a nice polo shirt, and I could smell his cologne pretty much from the second he walked into the shop.

"So you will never believe what just happened," he said.

"Tell me all about it!"

"Eddie just asked me for my number!"

My cheeks were warm. "Oh. Really?"

"Yeah, I guess I was right this whole time about the free coffee thing, except it wasn't you, it was me!" He was grinning.

"Well, what did you say?" I asked hoping he politely turned the cute barista down.

"I gave it to him," he replied flippantly. "He's cute. I'd totally take him out."

Growing up my mom always told me that I needed to be careful about my facial expressions. When I was in elementary school I would be sent to the office multiple times a week for rolling my eyes or frowning when someone said something I didn't like.

"You're very expressive," she would tell me. "And that's okay. It's a good thing. But there is a place to show your emotions and there is a place to hide them."

This is one of those times where I should not have let my expressions speak for me, but my face disagreed because David was already apologizing for being stupid and not thinking about what he was saying.

"He's cute but that doesn't mean I want to date him, I was just being polite," he argued while I was packing the book into my backpack. "Come on please talk to me. I came here today for you. I want to talk to you."

"David, I came here so we could try to make this work. I want to make things with you work. I want it so bad. I want to not feel like I made a huge mistake by losing you."

"I get that and I want the same…"

"You don't though," I said, my tone getting more and more annoyed. "We break up and within weeks you're sleeping with some gono' boy, and then you give it to me in a Taco Bell parking lot."

"I know and I said I was sorry for that but come on-"

"I'm not done yet," I interrupted him, my voice growing louder. "And then you come over to my place again just assuming that I want to sleep with you, and you say you're sorry and you cry in my arms and now you're going to do the same thing to the barista boy over there. And you're going to *brag* to me about it? Like I'm your best gal friend?"

The entire room was looking at us now. I was standing over David, still in his chair. He tried to say something but the words were stuck in his throat.

I still had plenty to say and had no problem saying any of it. But I wasn't going to waste any more of my time.

"I hope you figure out," I said gesturing at him in a circular motion, "whatever all of this is."

And then I left.

Dating App

I watched the glass of my phone as the square-shaped icon loaded an app onto my device. When it finished loading and the dull colors became fully vibrant, I hesitated to open it. A dating app. Something I hadn't tried before. But my friend, Jon, had just used this app to meet the man that he is now dating. So, I figured what's the worst that could happen?

I clicked on the icon and my phone turned black, only the small green logo in the center of the screen. It asked me for a username and a password, a photo of myself, what I was looking for specifically, and some general age and height stats.

My fingers felt heavy as I typed the words into the text boxes and uploaded photos of myself that had been pre-approved by Jon, and soon, I had an entire profile set up.

It felt strange to me that this was the new normal way to meet people. As if parties or nights out or introductions by mutual friends could no longer cut it.

The main screen of the app looked like an early 2000's chat room. A list of profiles like a ladder down the side with an option to "chat" or "wave."

"Now what do I do?" I asked Jon who was sitting sideways on the chair across from me at the bar.

"What do you mean," he said. "You just look through and talk to someone you think is cute."

"You know, I really don't think this is for me. I mean like how do you actually get to know someone through something like this. It feels impersonal."

"Ugh," he started in his complaining voice. "Why does everything have to be so serious with you?"

I closed the app and set my phone on the table. My face fell into my hands. At this point, I had been single for so long that dating didn't even feel like it was worthwhile. I took a sip of my gin and tonic.

"This is exactly why this is for you. I think you need this," he said. "Just chill out. Chat with some guys and don't take everything so personal. Just have a good time. It doesn't have to be love."

"I just don't see the point," I said as my phone vibrated on the table. A new message notification. "Why should I even read it?"

"Because you deserve to have some fun for once."

I didn't like it. But I thought maybe Jon was right. Maybe it had been too long since I let loose a little. I slide my finger across the screen of my phone and opened the app to see what was in store for me.

Date One

I sat alone at a table in a bar I had never been to. Dimly lit chandeliers and booming music, I was nervous that he wouldn't be able to find me in the dark storm of a dive.

We had plans to meet at 7pm but I was always annoyingly early and was sitting at the table by a quarter till. My collared shirt freshly pressed, my strawberry hair gelled in a swoop and I actually went and bought an expensive smelling cologne all to make a good first impression.

Coming into this date I think I was somewhat excited but mostly terrified. There were just too many outcomes to meeting someone you know nothing about. What if he looked nothing like his pictures? What if he chewed with his mouth open? What if he tried to kill me? It seemed pretty far-fetched, I know, but we have all heard those stories.

The music in the old bar took a turn to a slow and steady romantic song, and like out of a movie, I saw him walking towards me. Jason with his blonde hair that hung down by his ears and glittery green eyes that stood out from across the room. He looked almost more attractive than his pictures on the app.

He approached the table, smiled, and quizzically asked if I was who he thought I was.

"I am him," I said and smiled. "I hope I look how my pictures look!"

"You look exactly like I thought you would," he said with a shy laugh. "So nice to meet you in person!"

"Good! Same to you," I said. "Please have a seat. The server came by but I told him I'd wait till you got here to order a drink."

"How polite of you," he said smiling.

"It's a Midwesterner thing," I said with a wink. "New Yorkers like yourself usually say we are too polite."

When the server swung back around he took our drink orders. I asked for a gin and tonic as per usual and Jason got a mule. We decided to order a chips and salsa appetizer to share.

"So," Jason started as soon as we had our drinks in hand. "What is it that you looking for?" I was shocked at how casual he was about such a big question, and so early in the evening. But I guess better to get it out of the way, instead of wasting any time.

"Um, wow okay!" I said laughing. "I, um, I don't have any super specifics, but I know that I want to go on dates and find someone that I can have a solid relationship with. Someone to travel with. Someone to go to concerts with. Um, someone to eventually become more." I was starting to ramble so decided to stop and turn the question back on him.

"I'm looking for something similar," he said. "It's so hard to meet good people who want more than a one night fling." It's like he was reading my mind.

"I feel that too," I said. "Especially in the gay community…and in such a big city." He nodded in agreement.

The sounds of New York roared outside the bar. Taxis honking, people yelling, firetrucks speeding down the crowded streets. I never thought that I'd live here, but it definitely became a dream come true when I first stepped off the airplane three years earlier just three days after graduating college.

Four drinks into the evening and I was internally laughing at myself for feeling so nervous about this date. It had been much easier than I thought it would be. Jason was wonderful. He made me laugh, and the conversations felt equal. I never felt like when I was talking he was waiting to say what he wanted to say. He listened to me and I listened to him and together, we got to know each other.

He was an only child, which was a wild contrast to my four older siblings and seven nephews. His favorite color was purple, the same as mine. His music taste varied but has a strong love for alternative indie. And if he was stranded on an island, he would bring the Harry Potter series with him.

"Can I bring the whole series?" He asked. "Or do I have to pick one?"

"Oh good question," I said. "I have no idea. Well, wait. I say you can bring the whole series only if I can also bring seven books."

"I think that might be cheating," he said laughing.

"I don't make the rules, promise."

From start to finish, the evening went smoothly. And when it was time to go, we hovered around the front of the bar for just a few more moments before going our own ways.

"I had a nice time tonight," I said. "I was honestly so nervous about this but I think it went really well."

"I agree," he said. "We have to do this again sometime."

"I'd love that."

"I can't wait for you to meet Cameron. He is going to love you."

"Oh yeah" I felt my stomach drop just a little. "Wait, who is Cameron?"

"My boyfriend," he said casually. My head began to pound.

"We have both been going on dates because we want to add a third to our relationship. You really would just fit so perfectly."

I stood there in silence for a moment, staring at him, wondering at which point in our brief chat on the app and long conversations that evening I had given him any idea that that was what I was looking for.

"Ahhh, I am uh, I'm just gonna go. It was nice meeting you." And as I turned I swear my eyes rolled so hard they almost fell out of my head. I pulled my phone out, opened up the dating app and went to Jason's profile. Delete.

And then I walked home.

Date Two

After such a wonderful, and then weird, night with Jason, I wasn't completely sure why I agreed to go on another date from the app. But a guy named Brandon with tan skin and quirky framed glasses said hello and I couldn't help but say it back.

Another date at another dimly lit and loud bar. Why was I doing this to myself? I showed up right on time this time around and sat alone at a table while I waited for him.

In my head, I was giving myself mini pep talks to help me get through the evening. I had learned a lesson the last time. People aren't always going to be exactly who they say they are, and maybe that's okay. I had to look at myself here and decide if even my own profile on the app made me out to be exactly who I was, and not just the parts of myself I wanted people to see.

Ten minutes went by and Brandon still hadn't shown up, but I didn't feel bothered yet. Ten minutes could mean that he was stuck in traffic, and not necessarily that I was being stood up.

At the twenty-minute late mark, I sent Jon a text message, "Brandon still hasn't shown, remind me why I am doing this again?"

"Relax," he responded. "He is probably just running late. Take a lap around the bar. Maybe he is already there waiting for you too."

"Valid point," I typed back and then stood to see if I could find him maybe sitting at a table behind a pillar or in a dark corner. Maybe he was also sitting nervously, thinking it was me who was standing him up.

I walked to each corner of the bar and looked around in all the crevices that could potentially be hiding a patiently waiting patron. I checked my app and didn't have any messages from him. Maybe I was being stood up?

I walked across the bar once again and then down a hallway that led to the restrooms. I wasn't really sure what my plan was at this point but I thought it was worth a shot.

I stopped in my tracks when I saw him though. At first, I

wasn't completely sure, but when I saw the glasses I just knew. At the end of the hallway was Brandon, pushed up against the wall, another man pushed up against him, their mouths connected and hands running all over each other's bodies.

Maybe I should have shown up earlier than right on time. Maybe he got bored waiting. Once again, and without my control, my eyes rolled and I deleted yet another potential suitor from the dating app.

Date Three

I wasn't going to make the bar date mistake again. If I was going to go on a third date, it would be for lunch, in a well-lit restaurant. Or maybe even coffee. No more bars, though, I told myself. And that's what I told Alex when he messaged me and asked me out on a date.

He sat across the table from me at a lunch spot I'd never been to but the patio seemed nice enough for a first date. He smiled and told me about how his morning had been so far. How he too had been on some bad bar dates and understood wanting to meet in the daylight.

I felt at ease to be completely honest. Alex was easy to talk to. He had a nice smile with shiny white teeth. He wore casual clothing and was an elementary school teacher. And I mean, who was nicer and easier to get along with than someone who teaches small children?

"How long have you been in the city?" he asked me.

"For three years now. Moved here from Indiana and I don't think I'll ever go back."

"I totally get it. I moved here from California...things move to slowly there. I need the high energy and bustle."

"I understand. Indiana is suffocating at times."

The patio was starting to get busier as the official noon lunch hour was approaching, but we didn't mind. Stuck in our own little world of conversations about life and work and the hilariously bad dates we had been on.

"So what do you do for fun?" He asked me.

"I like going to concerts. Movies. I try to travel a few times a year to a new place. I might drink too much wine alone in my apartment, but I won't make that a definite trademark of my personality just yet. I love scrabble." He was smiling with approval. "What about you?"

"I also like movies and concerts and travel. I go to the gym daily to start my day. Do you go to the gym?"

"I don't have a gym membership. I mostly go for jogs around Central Park for exercise."

"I see," he said.

Something about the way his tone changed rubbed me the wrong way, but I shook it off. I was in no way out of shape, as if that should even matter. I mean I wasn't incredibly fit like he was, but I wasn't unfit either.

"I've enjoyed getting to know you today," he said. "I think you're cute and sweet and obviously very intelligent."

"Thank you," I said smiling. "I have enjoyed this too."

"I'd like to see you again, but I do think you should consider getting a gym membership. I usually only date healthy, fit guys."

I was dumbfounded. Unable to put together a sentence in my head. Was I that out of shape? Enough that someone I had just met would feel confident to point it out to me? I mean honestly, did I care what he thought? No. But that didn't make his statement any less appalling.

"Oh," I said. "I didn't realize I was unhealthy and out of shape?"

"Well maybe you're not unhealthy, but you could definitely stand to be more in shape."

"Uh…" I tried to string words together but my brain was at a total loss. I pulled out my wallet and laid cash out on the table to pay for my meal and drink. "I, ah, I hope you have a nice rest of your day, okay?"

"Oh, I have offended you haven't I? I mean it in a nice way I swear to you I do."

"I'm okay actually. Thank you though," I said and once again my eyes rolled as I walked away from another horrible date.

I pulled my phone out, and instead of only deleting Alex, I hard-pressed the app and deleted it from my phone altogether.

I woke late the next morning to a text from Jon, "What time can I pick you up for the party today?" I forgot I had committed to going. It was Sunday. I wanted to lie in bed all day.

"I can be ready in an hour," I said knowing I could get ready in thirty minutes but needed a little more time on my pillow.

"Okay. How did your date go?"

"I don't want to talk about it," I typed and hit send.

I sat down in the shower while the hot water drowned me. I felt stupid for thinking that after almost four years of dating no one, that I could jump right in and find the love of my life. Is that even what I wanted? Maybe I was just looking for some excitement. If that was all I was trying to find, I had definitely found it.

When I got to the party full of people who were Jon's friends but only casual acquaintances with me, I didn't feel like socializing. I had changed my shirt at least four times that morning, and still I didn't feel comfortable in my skin.

I sat alone in a big chair in the corner of the room and people watched. I admired how everyone seemed to feel comfortable. How everything flowed, and I wished I could just do the same.

A boy in funky blue pants and a t-shirt approached me and sat on the arm of my chair. "Hey there," he said confidently. "What're you doing over here all alone?"

"Oh, I'm just you know, ahh, people watching. I'm not feeling too social today, I guess." His eyes were a piercing cerulean and he had a long lean torso and bouncy curls on top of his head.

We introduced ourselves and chatted through the rest of the event. We flirted over cups of sangria and at the end of the day, we exchanged numbers.

"I hope to hear from you," he said to me in front of the apartment complex. "I had a nice time with you today."

"I had a nice time too." We hugged and when we moved to walk our own ways we found ourselves walking in the same direction.

"Oops!" He said with a laugh. "Where about do you live?"

"On 10 and 43," I said. "You?"

"I'm three blocks up," he said. "Come on I'll walk with ya."

He took my hand, and I blushed the entire twenty-block walk home.

Hope Is A Heartache

Taylor giggled as she leaned back from kissing Trevor on the lips. I stood there shocked, but then joined in on the laughter. I had never seen Taylor so drunk, but she was my favorite human after a few gin and tonics.

My usual drink of choice was tequila, but tonight I was drinking beer only for the fact that I had too much tequila the night before. So did they, but I wasn't as brave as them.

I met Taylor and Trevor at a coffee shop when I first moved to the city. They were at the table next to me chatting and laughing while I was working on an article for work. I don't remember what it was that made me feel brave enough to say hi, but I did, and we have been close ever since.

"I think you need a kiss too!" Taylor said walking towards me.

"Oh no, I don't think--," I said but before I could stop her she grabbed both of my cheeks with her gloved hands and kissed me right on the lips. I laughed but honestly I felt uncomfortable.

Not uncomfortable in that I didn't know or trust Taylor enough to kiss her in a joking way, more that I was, these days, uncomfortable in almost any situation. I was anxious. All of the time. Something to do with a new city and spending all of my time on two people I didn't know well enough to know whether or not they would be there if life unraveled.

And that's when it happened. In a quick moment that I did not expect even a little bit, Trevor grabbed my cheeks and planted his own kiss on me. I froze still, then relaxed, and felt it.

His lips were soft compared to mine, which were inevitably always chapped at that time of year. We stood there, suspended in a moment, his bare hands on my cheeks and our lips lightly pressed together.

Taylor's cackle pulled us apart and Trevor joined in on the laughter. After a moment, I started laughing as well.

It was odd because I had never seen Trevor as anything more than just a person I was friends with. We had met six months earlier and he was already my best friend. We had an undeniable chemistry as friends. And even before I knew for a fact that he was exclusively into women, I hadn't seen him as anything more than just another guy I was friends with.

On the car ride home, I sat in the back seat so I could avoid Taylor and Trevor. I didn't want them to see the emotion in my face, because if they asked me what was wrong, I wouldn't have known what to tell them.

A song that I had never heard scratched through the speakers of the old car and I stared out the window. Christmas lights on buildings passed in a blur and I decided maybe I should have just gone home for the holiday. Splurged on a plane ticket to get me out of this city that wasn't treating me the way I thought it would.

"You okay?" Taylor asked making eye contact with me in the smudged rear view mirror.

"Yeah, I'm okay." I replied. "Just tired."

"Do you wanna stay at my place?" Trevor asked. "So you don't have to do the walk?"

Trevor lived just a fifteen minute walk across a huge park from me, and Taylor lived in the opposite direction. So she normally dropped us off at Trevor's and then I would walk home. It was my idea because I liked taking walks at night. Especially this time of year when the park was lit up with a kaleidoscope of holiday lights.

"Sure," I replied to Trevor's offer. It wasn't a weird idea for me to stay at his apartment. I had done it multiple times before when my roommate was getting on my nerves or I if I had a little too much to drink.

The first time I fell asleep on his couch, which was honestly a sad excuse for a piece of furniture. I told him I'd never sleep on the lumpy mess again and from then on he always offered the other half of his king sized bed, and even then I never thought of him as more than just a friend.

Except tonight as he changed into his pajamas, and I pulled off my jeans I couldn't help but think what might happen. Was that random kiss actually not so random? Was it done on purpose? To send a message to me. He always knew I was gay and I always appreciated how accepting he was and how normal I felt around him. Because I never had a straight guy friend that made me feel like I was simply one of the guys.

Even in college my guy friends would make it a point to not change in front of me or to make jokes about how I couldn't change a tire or throw a ball, even though I could do all of those things, and probably better than them.

"Goodnight," Trevor yawned as he cuddled with himself under the covers.

"Night," I said laying there staring straight up at the white ceiling with pipes that ran every way. I laid there awake knowing that Trevor was already fast asleep but still wondering if maybe this could go somewhere. Have I had feelings for him this entire time that I was just suppressing? And an unsolicited kiss was the thing that dragged the feeling to the surface?

I had to turn it off. I had to take the feelings and shove them back down into the crease of my brain where they came from. I rolled onto my side and pulled a cover over myself. The alcohol was still making my head spin, and slowly, I fell asleep.

I woke up the next morning alone, still in Trevor's bed but with an extra blanket than what I fell asleep with. He worked early on weekdays and my job allowed me to work from home on my laptop, so often he would let me sleep in while he got ready at his six am wake up call.

I slid back into my jeans and made myself a cup of coffee. I envied Trevor that he was able to live alone, even if his entire apartment was smaller than my bedroom. I'd give up the extra space to not have to share a kitchen and bathroom with another person.

The place was a mess but I loved it. While my bedroom walls were blank, his were full from edge to edge with band posters and New Yorker magazine covers. At least fifteen pairs of old Chuck Taylors hanging by their shoe laces from the pipes that run across the living room ceiling, and a wall dedicated entirely to books.

I thought about how easily I could see myself in this place, living side-by-side with Trevor. Legs intertwined while reading our books on the lumpy couch. Him some over-complicated book that I would call pretentious and me with a romance novel that he would call simple.

Somehow I could create this whole life for me and him. I could see it so clearly in my head. Something that would never happen, and it terrified me. How could I fall for my straight best friend in a single night?

Later that day when I finished my work I sent a text message to Taylor and Trevor in our group chat to see if they had dinner plans. I had a weird work day and I didn't want to be home alone.

"I know a new spot on 10th ave!" Taylor responded. "Let's try it!"

"Sounds good to me. Trevor you in?"

"I can't tonight," Trevor texted. "I actually have a date tonight."

I was caught off guard. To the point where my feelings were almost hurt. As if Trevor was actually someone I had a chance with and he was turning me down.

"Oooooh, Trevor's got a hot date!" Taylor sent. "Maybe if it goes to shit you can meet us after!"

"That's great!" I lied, "But yeah maybe meet us after."

Dinner with just Taylor was different but maybe a nice change of pace. We sat at the bar of this new Italian restaurant and looked over the menus. The server offered us free wine samples, and even though we both had to work early, we decided to split a bottle.

Halfway through our appetizer and I was already feeling the buzz. Taylor's cheeks were rosy and everything made me feel giggly. We talked about our days and what our plans were for the Christmas which was just a week away. Taylor is from New Jersey, so she was lucky just have a short drive across the Hudson to be with her family.

"I didn't want to splurge on a plane ticket to only be in Chicago for just a few days," I said. "And Trevor felt the same about Ohio, so we decided to just stay here and watch movies and drink and whatever. I don't know. It should be fun."

"You okay?" She asked with concern. Like she could tell I

was falling apart and wanted to help.

"Yeah, totally," I said which only gave away that I was, in fact, not okay.

Taylor leaned forward towards me and put her elbows on the table. Her face was serious. She could see right through me.

"It's okay if you like him," she said. "It's okay to have feelings for him. Just don't let it consume you. Feel them, and then move on."

I sank in my chair. My whole body was heavy in the moment and I was starting to regret the wine.

I tried to find words of denial. To tell her she's seeing things that aren't there. Trevor would never want me. Not in the way that I wanted him to, but he was still my best friend. My person. Who I told all my secrets to. I hoped that even if it was obvious to Taylor what I was feeling, that it wasn't obvious to Trevor as well.

After dinner we decided to go for a walk and see what bars we could find with a happy hour. The evening air was cold on my cheeks and so I buried my face into my scarf hoping the wind wouldn't reach me.

We turned the corner and passed a bar that had large floor to ceiling windows. You could see clear across the entire bar that was decorated with Christmas lights and fake garland. I admired the attention to detail.

"Hey, is that Trevor?," Taylor asked. I squinted through the window and there he was. Slouched in a chair like he always was. Smiling while the brunette sitting across from him was talking. Dramatically using her arms around as she spoke. He smiled harder and there was a twist in my stomach.

"Yeah, that's him on his date," I said plainly.

"Oh…" Taylor said. "Come on we can go."

"No hold on," I said. I wasn't sure what I thought staying would help. Maybe It was that if I saw how impossible it would be to love him, then I wouldn't. Maybe simply seeing him so happy made me feel happy. I don't know what it was, but it did feel necessary for just that moment. And right as I was about to turn away, he saw me. Locked his eyes on mine in through the window, and I couldn't move. His eyes were saying something that I couldn't quiet translate. They were sad? Maybe regrettable? A feeling I had never felt from Trevor was being sent from him to me across the restaurant and through the glass.

"Okay let's go," Taylor said pulling me. I watched and Trevor shook his focus back into the woman that was sitting across from him.

"Okay," I said letting her gain the leverage to pull me from the window. "Can we find some tequila?"

We walked another street over to a dive that Taylor would frequent. Upon entry you were given a rose and they had an actual jukebox with old vinyl.

"What're you thinking?" Taylor asked me. My mind was wandering from one end of the bar to the other and all the way back to the window where Trevor and I locked eyes.

"I'm unsure," I replied.

"I'll go get us some shots," she said. "Do you work tomorrow?"

"Yeah but I might use a vacation day."

"Ohhh, yeah do that!" She said.

I sat there alone at a table while Taylor went to order us a round of shots. Checking my phone constantly hoping that maybe Trevor's date would end early and he could join us. Hoping that maybe the look he had on his face wasn't one of negativity but a positive and happy intention. Hoping that maybe he'd call me and ask me to stay the night with him.

By our third shot I was more than tipsy and still there was no text or call from Trevor. And as I ordered another round from the bartender, all I could think was that hope is a heartache and I am full of it.

When I woke the next morning my head was pounding. Another night with too many shots of tequila in the books, and I knew that I probably only had a few left in me before I completely collapsed.

Thankfully, work had approved my vacation day so I was able to sleep in and not worry about anything but feeling better. Not only was my brain dead from too many shots of tequila, but also my ego was throbbing from the run in with Trevor. What was that look he gave me?

An hour later I woke again to my phone ringing. The sound echoed around my small New York apartment. I stood and wandered around the wintery cold room searching for my phone. Lifting up couch cushions and papers on the desk. I walked into the bathroom and found it in the sink right as the ringing stopped.

The screen read that I had two missed calls from Trevor. I looked at my bed head and droopy sad eyes in the mirror. New York wasn't wearing well on me. I had been drinking more than ever before and staying out late almost every night, getting only minimal hours before having to be up for work. My beard was overgrown and I was breaking out on my forehead.

My phone started to ring again. Trevor's name and photo lit the screen. I slid my thumb across the glass to answer.

"Hello?" I said with a crack in my voice. I cleared my

throat., "Hello? Sorry I just woke up."

"Hey, all good," Trevor said into the phone quickly. Quietly. He almost sounded sad or ashamed. "Are you free to meet for a coffee? I need to talk to you about something."

My head pounded harder. What could he need to talk about so urgently? Did Taylor tell him about last night? Did she tell him I had feelings for him? After all, she did know him at least a few years compared to the few months that I've known him. It would only make sense for her to confide in him and take his side in all of it.

"Um," I struggled to string any words together. "Uh, yeah sure? I can be at our normal spot in, ahhh, 45 minutes?"

"That's perfect. I'll see you there." He said and hung up.

Twenty minutes later and after throwing up twice, I was walking the three blocks to the hole in the wall coffee shop where I had originally met Trevor. My head was still slightly angry with me for my night out but at least my stomach was feeling better.

When I arrived at the coffee shop I could see Trevor already sitting at a table, coffee in hand. I stopped at looked for a moment, reminiscing on the night before when I saw him with his date. Something about the way he looked at me still gave me chills.

I walked in the door, ordered my usual mocha latte, and sat down across from him, "Hey there," I said. My hands were clammy.

"Hey," he said. "How are you?" I wanted to tell him I felt like my insides were on the outside. That I had drank so much the night before to forget my feelings for him. That he was the only thing I could ever think about.

"I'm doing okay. A little hungover so I decided to take a vacation day."

He shifted uncomfortably in his seat. I still had no idea what was about to come from him, and I still felt completely terrified of it.

"So I need to tell you something," he started. "But I am really struggling with it so please, please be patient and work with me here."

"Okay…" I said. "I promise." He shifted again and laid his face into his hands.

"I'm just feeling things…that I have never felt before and I can't get it out of my head," he said. "I can't think right because of it. It's consuming me. And it took me a long time to even realize what it was because like I said it is such a foreign feeling to me."

I sat there stunned by the words that were coming from his lips. I had never seen Trevor in such a state of anxiety. Normally, Trevor was calm and cool and collected, but now he was fumbling over himself barely able to make a complete sentence.

"So anyway, and it took me a minute but last night when I saw you through the window it really finally just, erm ya know, it really just hit me," his foot was tapping aggressively on the floor of the coffee shop, shaking the entire table and our hot drinks. "But anyway, I don't really know what any of it means as of now but it's how I feel…do you understand?"

I sat still for a moment, and kept silent. Then said, "Trevor, you never said what you are actually feeling."

"Isn't it obvious?" He said and I gave a sympathetic shrug, "You're really going to make me say it. Okay, um, I have feelings. And they are big feelings, not friendly feelings, and I have them…for you."

It took everything in me to keep from my face twisting. Was this some kind of a joke? Surely it couldn't be. He was too nervous. Too afraid to say it. There is no way he would make a joke like this, or at my expense.

"Trevor I-"

"I know. I know. It's crazy!" He started again, "and I wasn't sure if I should even tell you or not because, well because, I know that you only have platonic feelings for me and I didn't want to ruin the dynamic of our friendship by saying all of this." He paused for a moment, "but it was eating at me, and once I figured it out, I couldn't not talk to you about it...you're my best friend."

"Well Trevor actually-"

"Oh my gosh, I am so sorry," he interrupted me. "I shouldn't have said anything. Please don't tell anyone and we can completely just forget we ever had this conversation, okay? I mean is that even possible to just-"

"Trevor stop talking," I said. "Please stop, I am trying to tell you that I have feelings for you too."

He sunk in his chair, "Oh. You do?"

"I do...and it took me a minute too, but I figured it out the night that you kissed me as a joke."

"It wasn't a joke," he said. "I guess I used the situation to my advantage...to test myself...but it wasn't a joke."

I smiled shyly and took a sip of my coffee to hide it. While Trevor and I sat here in a moment of extreme realization, the rest of the world around us in that coffee shop went on without a care.

Baristas calling names and drinks echoed through the shop. Business men and women in a scurry to add milk and sugar to their reusable travel mugs before running to catch a subway to work.

"Would you like to go for a walk?" Trevor asked. "It's actually not freezing today. I even pulled out my light jacket." I looked down at myself, still in sweats, a hoodie, and a hat to hide my bed head.

"Sure," I replied. "Can we stop at my place so I can put real pants on first?"

"Of course," he said with a smile and a wink. I truly couldn't believe what was happening.

After I changed and ran a comb through my hair, and we went for a walk through the neighborhood. Trevor was right when he told me I wouldn't need more than a light jacket. The sun was burning as it shined down from straight above, melting the piles of snow. Not what I expected in New York in December but Trevor assured me it was somewhat common.

We talked more about his date and the moment his true feelings hit him. I told him how I'd been feeling a simultaneous feeling of hope and hopelessness for a couple of weeks. Both of us always wanting to say something but afraid to ruin a friendship that had grown so strong so quickly.

"So," I started as we turned a corner. "Does that mean you are bi-sexual then?"

"Hmm," he said. "I don't know? I don't know what to call it if I usually like girls, and only one guy? I don't know." I could tell he was frustrated with his confusion. I was confused and frustrated for such a long time myself.

Endless days in middle and high school where I knew I was different but didn't understand how or why. Dealing with guys from my grade making fun of me, calling me names in the locker room, pushing me over and kicking me because apparently they knew better than I did. And they knew it was wrong. It took me years to come back from those things, and I felt relief that Trevor wouldn't have to go through them.

"Well you know what?" I said. "The good thing is that what you label yourself holds no merit to who you are as a person. It doesn't matter. As long as you know what you like and you feel comfortable with it, then that is all that matters."

"Thanks," he said with a smile. "That really helps me, I think. People get so caught up in it."

"I understand why some people do. I think it is important for some people to really understand and be able to tell themselves exactly who they are, and for others it isn't so important. Coming out and telling people like 'hey this is me. I am a gay man' was therapeutic for me in a way. It helped me come to terms with it. And it helped me overcome all of the shit I had to go through when I was younger."

It was strange to me how comfortable I felt talking about these topics with Trevor. Topics I had barely even discussed with my parents or siblings, or even thought about myself, were pouring out of me like they meant so little. It was different that for a moment I was the confident one that was teaching Trevor how to relax in a feeling, and not the other way around.

"I appreciate you sharing that with me," he said. "I have truly loved getting to know you more and more over the past few months. I mean it when I say that you are my best friend."

"You're mine too," I replied.

"Wanna come and watch a movie or something?" he asked. "A nice walk and a movie. We can consider this our first official date."

We sat on opposite sides his lumpy couch in his small apartment. I wanted to pull him in and lie down with his body against mine, but I knew that I would need to take things slow with him. That I would need to watch for his signals and make sure he was completely comfortable before I made any moves.

Going on dates with boys who *might* be completely straight wasn't something that I liked to make a habit of. Something about the fragility of it always made me anxious. I would never forget when I was in college, half naked on my couch with a boys tongue in my mouth. He was "curious" and picked me to help with his sexual hypothesis.

We weren't even our of our pants before he stopped, looked me right in the eyes, and told me he wasn't feeling the situation quite as much as he thought he would. Then he got up and left. And while I knew that it didn't actually have anything to do with me, and everything to do with the fact that he was really just straight, my ego still took a blow.

I watched Trevor as he scrolled through Netflix trying to find a movie for us to enjoy for our first official date, and I couldn't believe it. Our first official date. His words, not mine.

We settled on an original Christmas movie that really was probably too corny for my liking but the movie really didn't matter to me. I just wanted to sit beside Trevor and get to know him in this brand new way. A way that made our hands lock and our bodies touch and live in a completely beautiful and vulnerable place.

I could feel my heart getting ahead of my head. I had to give myself constant reminders that this could still go terribly wrong. For both of us. It could ruin a friendship. Or I could get hurt, and Trevor could walk away unscathed. Could I handle losing my only true friend in this city?

Trevor removed the cushions from the back of the couch and pulled me by my waist to lay with him while we watched the movie. His breath on the back of my neck made my body relax and all my of worries became small.

Maybe this could kill me, but I supposed so could anything that was truly worthwhile.

That Saturday I met Taylor for coffee and debated on whether or not I should tell her. I mean, she was my friend after all. But she was a friend to Trevor long before I came around. I felt too excited though to hold it in.

It had been three days since we confessed our feelings for each other in the coffee shop and besides when we were at work, we had spent almost every minute together since.

"So," I said shyly to Taylor who was sitting across from me flipping through a book. "I think I have something to tell you. But I am kind of torn if I should or not." She closed her book without marking her spot and leaned in towards me.

"Does it have to do with the past three days you've spent with Trevor?" she asked me with a wink.

"What?" I said with sarcasm. "He told you?"

"Of course he did. We are best friends. We share everything with each other."

I honestly felt some kind of a relief. Not only was Trevor holding my hand and holding me through the night, but he also felt confident enough to share the experience with his closest friends.

"Can I be honest with you?" Taylor said in tone serious enough to make me anxious.

"I always want you to be honest."

"I feel...happy about this...but also nervous...specifically for you."

I leaned back in my chair. Unsure of how to respond, and I think it was because, and I didn't want to admit it, but I was also nervous for myself. Even when I was lying beside Trevor with his arms wrapped around me, I still felt anxious. Vulnerable even, because he held all of the power, didn't he?

"I can feel it too," I admitted. "It feels like…like everything could be taken away from me at any moment."

"I hate to say it," she started. "But I have seen this situation play out before. Not with Trevor, of course, but with other friends. It hardly ever works."

I took a long sip from my mug to give myself time to think of a response. She was right and even though some part of me knew she was, I didn't want to believe it.

"I know how it can seem that way," I said. "And I have been thinking about that constantly for the past few days since he admitted to me his feelings. I just don't know how to be smart about this, ya know? Like I don't know how to not pursue this to the fullest extent."

"I know," she said sympathetically. "I think it's one of those things that you have to go into full force and maybe you'll end up hurt, but maybe you won't. I don't think there is anything else you can do."

I let her words sink in. I felt thankful to have someone like Taylor around to talk me through this, and I hoped that she would be doing the same for Trevor.

The next day while I was at work, I got a text from Trevor, "Wanna go with me to a party tonight? I have an old friend from college whose band is performing."

"Sounds good to me," I typed back. "What time are you thinking?"

"I'll swing by around 7? That way we can grab a drink beforehand? Taylor is coming too."

"Perfect. See ya then."

I sat at my desk and let my mind wander. For the first time in what felt like year, I felt confident in a relationship. I understood why Taylor had her doubts or worries, but ultimately, I think she's is reading the situation wrong. This wasn't just some random straight guy that didn't know me or care about my feelings. This was Trevor. My best friend. I trust that he wouldn't do anything to hurt me.

Not on purpose, at least.

We stood in a corner of the crowded dive bar. Light flickered shades of red and blue and purple across the walls and floors. With drinks in hand, we waited for Trevor's friend to come on.

"I've never seen Brian's band perform," Trevor said. "So don't get mad at me if they suck, okay?"

"I mean if they got a gig here they can't be awful," Taylor said. "I'm going to go get a round of tequila shots for us, sound good?" she asked and walked over to the bar without waiting for an answer. I stood next to Trevor, both in silence.

My mind raced with thoughts from my conversation with Taylor. He honestly hadn't really treated me much differently than he did before, so what if she was right? Our relationship had remained almost exactly the same, but with a different label on it. Dating. Was that even a label? Did that come with a commitment? Or was it something that two people just do? And is that what Trevor and I were doing? Or was it something that we were? Why was this difficult to decipher?

While my head was doing its back and forth and not making sense, Trevor stood beside me, and I assumed maybe he was going through the same motion of thoughts.

Taylor returned with three shots of what I guessed was the

cheapest tequila in the bar. Without waiting for a cheers, I took the shot and threw it back. The wretched taste reaching ever corner of my mouth and making my face twist.

"Wow," Taylor said and then threw back her own. "Looks like we need another round." Trevor tossed his back too and gave Taylor a twenty for the next round.

"I'm sorry things are weird right now," he said after Taylor walked away. "Are things weird? Do you feel weird?"

"I kinda do," I said. "I'm unsure. My brain is all over the place."

"Mine too," he said, and somehow he found the courage to reach for my hand. I pulled away quickly.

"Oh my god. I am so sorry I don't know why I did that." His eyes were sad as he tried to assure me it was okay.

"It's really okay," he said. "It's okay if you aren't interested. I understand."

"No it's not that I'm not interested," I said. "It's that I am so interested. And I am terrified that because you are straight or mostly straight or whatever you are that this could end up crashing down on me. Because I know so certainly what I want, but what if we are together and you change your mind?"

He took in the words I was saying, and my hands shook while I waited for a response.

"I understand," he said. "I know that it must be scary. And I know it might look like I am using you as an experiment. But I promise you it's not that."

"Okay," I said still uncertain with his intentions.

"Look," he started. "I can't make you any promises, but you can't make me any either. No one can. Relationships can start and end for a million different reasons, and the feeling you have now is just one of them. But I understand if you want to leave this alone."

"You're right. I'm sorry. It's different though isn't it?"

"I don't think that it is," he said as he reached for my hand again, but slower. I interlocked my hand in his and he placed a quick kiss on my cheek.

Taylor returned with another round of shots, and we cheered to a fun night. And as the band started their opening number I thought to myself, maybe hope is a heartache, but maybe this would be completely worth it.

L

I met Connor in an art class during the first semester of my junior year of high school but we didn't actually become friends until the following summer, when my cousin reintroduced us. Camille had always told me she thought the two of us would get along, but I don't think she realized it would be to the extent that we did.

It was awkward at first. Uncomfortable moments trying to make conversation. Me catching him staring at me or the other way around.

Looking back at it now you can't blame either of us. I can't speak for Connor, but even at seventeen, I didn't know what my feelings were towards people. I knew I liked girls, but there was a small part of me that was also intrigued by the idea of men.

It felt less like an attraction and more like a platonic bond. I would see guys and I'd be confused between whether I wanted to be friends with them, or if I wanted to be them. When it came to Connor though, I knew what I wanted, and it wasn't platonic.

I spent an entire summer sending him signs. Pretending that Connor was nothing more than a friend to me but always seeing what buttons I could push to make him notice me a little bit more. I spent months side-eyeing him and touching his hips lightly when I walked passed him. Small things that he might not have even noticed.

I finally gave up on him the beginning of our junior year

when he started dating a girl named Collette. I'd be lying if I said it didn't shock me. I thought my attempts on him were working, but I found myself wrong. Depressed in bed for an entire weekend over a relationship with Connor that never existed anywhere but in my own head.

I found a way to move on, and her name was Katrina. Katrina and I had known each other for a few years. There was always a small spark between us. A light in the dark tunnel of my mind, but of course with her, I was always questioning my intentions. Even when I was with Katrina, I still only ever thought of Connor.

Connor and Collette, and me and Katrina became inseparable. The four of us spent our weekends and evenings together sitting around bonfires, going to the movies, making dinners and desserts together, taking pictures and making videos.

It was the first day of autumn. The four of us were cuddled up under a mountain of blankets on Connors couch watching a movie about skiers stuck on a ski-lift overnight. A hand slid into mine under the covers. I thought it was Katrina until I felt the thick steel thumb ring that I knew belonged to Connor.

I looked over at him intending to make fun of him. I had assumed he was reaching for Collette, and in the mess of hands under the covers, accidentally found me. I looked over to him to turn the happening into a joke, and with Collette asleep on his shoulder, he was looking back at me.

I squeezed his hand and smiled. Shook my head at him so he could see his mistake. But instead of laughing and letting go, he gripped my hand harder and smiled a handsome flirtatious smile at me.

I knew it was wrong. I thought of Katrina and I wanted to pull away, but I couldn't. The nerves that connected my fingers through my heart and into my brain refused to let me let go, and I thanked them for it. I wanted him - and my heart and my mind would do whatever it took to get him.

Connor massaged my hand with his thumb and index finger. My hands were clammy and my cheeks were red. The movie ended. He let go, and I was drained of everything.

"Is it over already?" Katrina yawned.

"Yeah," I said with a smile. "You passed out before it even started. Like always."

She climbed up from the couch and checked her phone that was sitting on the coffee table, "Oh it's already ten, I've gotta go. Does anyone need a ride home?"

"Yeah that would be great," Collette answered.

I looked to Connor for an answer and instantly regretted it when his face was begging me to stay. There was no doubt in those green eyes. But I couldn't stay, could I?

"I think I'm going to hang out for a bit," I said. "I'll just walk home. I could use some fresh air."

"Okay, you sure?" She asked through another yawn.

"Yeah," I said with a fake smile. "I'm sure."

Connor and I sat cross-legged across from each other on his twin-sized bed. The room smelled like cheap aerosol cologne. We didn't say a thing. Just stared into each other's eyes. Fighting for the other to make the first move, even though, Connor already had by holding my hand under the covers.

I wanted him, I knew that, and even though I was sure he wanted me too, there was still a small inkling of doubt. Because how badly would our friendship be destroyed if I made a move and he didn't reciprocate. It could be catastrophic.

My fingers danced on the hem of my gym shorts. A nervous habit that my mom always scolded me for. Connor's hands rested still on his knees as though he was meditating. I admired his calm even in this emotional storm.

"I like you," he said finally. "I like you in a way that I can't understand. And sometimes, like earlier, I feel so brave, but other times, like right now, I feel like I could hit you for making me so confused."

"Oh," I said quietly, and now it was my turn to be brave. "I have wanted you since the day I met you in art class."

I moved my hand from my knee and rested it on his. I could feel his body relax and mine did too.

"Will you stay the night with me?" He asked. It was a school night but I said yes anyway, and without any words, Connor and I laid down in his bed. Side by side, my arms wrapped around him. No one else mattered.

One week, two weeks, three weeks had gone by and my sleepovers at Connor's were now a regular thing. Sometimes I would be too tired to go home after a date night with Collette and Katrina and sometimes I would sneak out to in the middle of the night and walk a mile in the pitch black to his house.

At first, it was just curiosity. We cuddled and talked but nothing more. It didn't feel like I was doing anything wrong because ultimately holding Connor through the night felt so right.

There was one night specifically when Connor's parents were out of town. We sat on the floor in front of the fireplace in our pajamas. Under a large grey blanket, with my head on his chest, Connor sighed and said, so quietly that I almost didn't hear him, "I think I am in love with you."

"I think I love you too."

I lifted my head, we sat up, and for the first time, I stopped fighting myself and finally, we brought our lips together.

The next day I broke up with Katrina, and I hate to say it, but it was one of the easier decisions I had to make. I loved Katrina but it wasn't a grow old together kind of love. More like a Meredith and Christina kind of love.

"Oh," she said. "I understand."

She was kind to me. I think even then she knew why it was happening. And I knew I would owe her my friendship forever.

Connor, on the other hand, wasn't ready to break up with Collette. And I loved him so much that I let him take his time. After all, it was only a kiss. We did make our way up to his bed but made the mutual decision to wait until we were both single to do anything more than just kiss.

For two more months, we continued seeing each other in secret. Sleepovers, sneaking out in the middle of the night for a make-out session, quick kisses in the hallway when we knew no one would see us. We were in love and being reckless with the feelings of those around us.

Time after time Connor tried to end things with Collette. Countless times he promised that today would be the day that he would end his relationship with Collette and come to me. He would tell me he felt brave and stronger and ready. Every time I would sit by my phone and wait for him to tell me he did it, but he never did. He'd call me crying and apologizing that he just couldn't do it.

Every day felt like a task. Every day came with a heaviness that sat hard on my neck and shoulders. Every day I got weaker. I'd lose sleep. My grades were falling. My relationships with my friends were fading away.

"Hey, I miss you," Camille said stopping me in the hallway one day after first period. "You never come around anymore, are you okay?" I only felt shame. I wanted to tell her. To fall apart in her arms and come clean, but I never did.

"Connor," I said one day when we were alone in his house. Once again under the covers in front of the fireplace, my head rested on his chest. "Connor, what are we even doing anymore?"

I could feel his heart beat faster. I could feel him losing his breath to find the right words to say, but he didn't.

"I am so exhausted of lying," I continued. "I need to know how long until I can stop lying. I am so tired."

We sat up and he said, "I can't do it. I can't break her heart."

"Right," I said with an eye roll. I stood and walked away from him. My hands rested on the kitchen counter and I hung my head while I thought of what to say next.

"Hey," he said stumbling over his words. "I'm sorry. Why can't things just stay the way they are? It's not like either of us are ready to come out yet anyway."

"It just isn't right Connor," I was gritting my teeth. "We can't keep doing this to Collette. We can keep our relationship a secret but it has to be just us."

Silence. Connor came and wrapped his arms around my waist from behind. His breath on the back of my neck. My body shivered. His touch was irresistible.

"I can't hurt her," he said into my neck.
"But what about me?" I said pushing his hands away from me, "I understand that you don't want to hurt Collette, but what about the pain I'm in? The stress I'm under?" My voice exhausted and desperate, and I was ashamed of it. Because even if Connor never broke up with Collette, I would still give him every single piece of me. I would run myself into the ground to make every day a day full of Connor.

He rested one hand on my shoulder and the other on my hip to spin me around towards him. I scanned his face for answers but found nothing but a boy who was just as lost as I was. Trapped between two lives, one that was praised and one that was looked down on.

I leaned in and kissed him on his cheek, and then again on his lips. And then again. He took my hand and led me to his room. Pulled off his shirt and then pulled my sweater over my head. We held each other and kissed. Under the covers, we slid out of the rest of our clothes.

His bare skin on mine. I felt greedy and selfish and anxious and happy and exhilarated and like nothing in this world could pull us apart. Because isn't that what love is when you're only seventeen?

It was the Saturday before Christmas. Connor, Collette, me, and our new friend, Theo, were spending the day together for a gift exchange. Theo was a foreign exchange student from Italy that was living with Connor for the second semester of our senior year, but he got here a month early to get ahold of American living.

Theo and I honestly didn't get along at first. I think maybe it was because he cut into my time with Connor. The fact that Connor's parents both had high power corporate jobs made it easy for us to have alone time at his house, but now Theo was always around, too.

Once I got over my petty distaste for him, I actually enjoyed his time. He was sweet in an innocent type of way and had interesting stories about all of the travels around Europe he had with his family.

The four of us sat in a circle, legs crossed with a pile of gifts in front of us, and we took turns opening them. Collette made the three of us a customized mixed CD. Theo had knit Connor and I both hats, and Collette a scarf. I gifted everyone a framed picture from when the four of us went ice skating at the beginning of the holiday break.

I picked up the gift with my name on it from Connor, and slowly, I pulled at the wrapping paper to reveal a hand-drawn and framed picture of me and him together. Big smiles, our arms wrapped over each other's shoulders. A photo that to anyone else would have looked like two best friends, but I knew better.

I leaned over to hug him and whispered in his ear, "Thank you so much for being you, and thank you for being mine."

Theo and Collette got similar presents from Connor, except in Theo's they were fist-bumping, which was cute and also somewhat awkward. It was the drawing that Collette got that struck a chord on me. The photo featured Connor and Collette sitting on a couch, hand in hand, and kissing each other.

It hurt my feelings only a little bit until she also leaned over and whispered into his ear. The idea of them having their own secrets. The idea of them having a life together that I wasn't a part of made me realize that maybe he was more hers than he was mine. That I would never have him as I needed him.

"This was so great, guys," Collette said. "I love all of these gifts."

"Yes, me too!" Theo added and I nodded to at least look like I agreed, when I just actually felt pathetic.

Collette nudged Connor and together they excused themselves from the living room and up the stairway to Connor's bedroom. I sat in broken silence. My cheeks and heart caught by the same fire.

Theo already had his headphones connected to his laptop listening to the CD that was made especially for him. He sat on the couch with his eyes closed, and I paced back and forth across the living room dreading the idea of whatever Collette and Connor may be doing right above me.

As I paced my anger fizzled into something quieter. It fizzled into pain. Anger is rarely just that. It's an emotion that blankets another emotion. A cover for your jealousy, or embarrassment, or sadness. And underneath my anger, I was feeling all of those things.

"Are you okay?" Theo said from his position on the couch.

"I'm fine," I snapped back at him.

"You are not fine. You are pacing and your eyes are wet," he said as he stood up and walked towards me. I lied that I was fine again, and it only pushed me further down because all I did anymore was tell lies.

Theo watched me as I paced, and even though I had been able to hide my true feelings for so long, this was my breaking point. He put his hands on my shoulders to stop me from pacing.

"Tell me what is wrong and I can help," he said. So clueless to how big of a lie I was living. I started to cry, and then I started to sob. I couldn't breathe, my stomach was twisted in a knot, and my hands were shaking aggressively. Theo tried to hug me but I held him away. I didn't want to ruin his night or be a burden. I didn't want him to ask me again what was wrong because then I'd have to lie and I was so exhausted of lying.

It was all I ever did anymore. To my friends, my parents, my siblings, to Collette, and the worst of all, to myself. I was a liar, and I was so good at it that it barely even phased me anymore.

So when he asked me again, I didn't give him an answer but I just cried harder and finally I let him pull me in. His arms wrapped around me tightly. I felt safe, even if just for a moment.

I stayed there paralyzed in his arms for several minutes before he finally loosened his grip. His hands moved from my lower back to my hips, sending a chill through my body and into the tips of my fingers. Then, as if from some romantic comedy, he looked me right in the eyes and he kissed me. Gently at first, as if to not startle me. He pulled my hips in closer to him, and he kissed me again. Longer and more passionate than the first time.

Something in me was telling me to push him away, that he was not the person I should be kissing. Another part was telling me to keep going. To take him back to his room and share with him what Connor was sharing with Collette. To fight fire with fire and hurt Connor the way that he was hurting me.

Theo took my hand and led me to his room. What used to be known as the guest room, was now full of personality. A map of Europe on the wall, framed photos of Theo and his family on the nightstand, strands of lights hanging around the room. He moved in and brought a whole life with him.

We laid on the bed facing each other, "Does anyone know?"

"Know what?" he asked.

"That you like guys."

"No," he said. "I never have until I met you."

I flipped over so that I was facing away from him. He leaned into me and wrapped his arm around me like I would do to Connor all those nights that I snuck through the window into his house. Theo held my hand and told me I could stay over if I wanted to.

"Collette stays over all the time so I don't think it's a big deal," he said and he pulled me in tighter.

"Oh," I said. "Sure."

"Goodnight, then."

"Yeah, goodnight," I said pressing my face into the pillow so he wouldn't hear that I was still crying.

I

I pushed Connor to the side, and it legitimately pissed me off that he couldn't figure out why I was doing it. We continued to hang out in our group, but I didn't give him any more attention than I thought would make it look suspicious.

On the other hand, Theo and I had a growing bond. Still, I kept him at arm's length. I enjoyed his time, but I did not want to lead him on.

It was Collette's idea that during the second semester we would all join the theatre together. We were all casts as extras in the musical Annie. I thought that theatre was fun but would have preferred any other show only to avoid all of the redhead jokes.

It had been almost two months since I stayed the night with Connor. Once Theo told me that Collette to stays over often, I didn't feel like he needed me anymore. Because as much as I wasn't reaching out, neither was he.

Maybe I pushed a little too hard and he let go. Maybe I punished him a little bit too much for being confused about what he wants, which is ultimately something none of us can control.

One day at rehearsal was especially stressful. There was a dance move where you had to spin around on your left foot and land on your right and for some reason, I just couldn't figure it out.

I watched Connor as he passed through the move like it was something he did every day. Usually, it was me that nailed the dancing and Connor would need extra help. But that day he was among the few to get it right, his face lit up with such beautiful happiness.

Is this what Connor's life looked like without me in it? Was he happier? Less stressed? Was I the thing that was making him miserable for the few months that we were sneaking around. Or was this happiness a well-played act?

I decided to talk to Connor that day after rehearsal. I would corner him if I had to, but I needed to figure out what was going on inside his head. Did he want Collette or did he want me?

I watched as he and Theo left the auditorium together. I was asked to stay a few minutes after to make sure I had the dance move perfected. Having the opportunity to talk to Connor before he left was motivation to get it right five times in a row, and my director released me.

I ran out of the auditorium and straight to the dressing room where I knew Connor would be changing out of his rehearsal clothes to go home. I felt a new sense of purpose. A new motivation to make a relationship with Connor my priority. To come clean to him about my kiss with Theo and why I had been distant throughout the past two months.

I pushed through the door of the dressing room and froze, my heart started pounding like a drum in my chest, beads of sweat falling down my forehead. Connor was pressed up against the wall, Theo pressed up against him, their lips pressed together. I tried to find words but, instead, stuttered and they looked over at me.

"Oh shit," Theo said. "No, it's not..." But he lost his words too. I took a step backwards towards the door I came through.

Theo called my name and took a step forward. I stepped back again. He looked confused. Saddened. Regretful. Like he knew that he had done something wrong. But I didn't think he did. Theo isn't the one who I was in love with, and he wasn't in a relationship with anyone else.

It was Connor that was poking holes in my chest, because there he stood in place, smiling at me. As if he were proud to be hurting me. My body was in physical pain. My head pounding, my heart racing.

I turned and I ran. Ran straight out of the room. Theo called for me again and I fought out a "No, it's fine. I'm fine."

The air felt thin and my cheeks were hot and my eyes were blurry. I ran through the halls of the school to get as far away from Theo and Connor as possible. I ran into the choir room and slammed the door behind me. Leaning on the wall to catch my breath.

A voice called my name. I opened my eyes to see Katrina sitting at the piano on the other side of the room, "Are you okay?" She asked standing and walking towards me. "Hey what's wrong? You can tell me."

I had an opportunity here to come clean. I fought myself internally if I should take it. Was telling Katrina what just happened even worse than lying? Did they deserve my loyalty? If you gave me even a second to consider the outcome, I would say they completely deserved my loyalty. This could destroy their lives. This could ruin every aspect of who they are. I can't out them just because I felt hurt, could I? "Tell me what's going on..." She said. "I can help."

I thought again about how Connor smiled when I caught them. How vengeful he looked. How satisfied with my pain. How pleased he looked to be evening the score. I took a deep breath, wiped my eyes with my shaking hands, and as plainly and as distant from the situation as I could, I said, "Connor is cheating on Collette with Theo."

"Tell me it isn't true. Tell me you were lying. Please tell me it was all a lie," Collette said to me through tears. I was in the middle of history class, but that didn't stop her from asking my teacher if she could borrow me for a minute. She was so pulled together that I didn't even know what was about to come.

"Please tell me you were angry or something so you lied about Connor and Theo being together."

I had regretted telling Katrina almost as soon as I did it. Especially since I had only given her half of the story. I didn't tell her about how Connor and I were in love, or how I also made out and spent the night with Theo myself. I threw Connor and Theo into oncoming traffic and walked away without a scratch.

I stood there paralyzed in fear. Once again I was given an opportunity to come clean. And I don't know what kept me from doing just that. I couldn't figure out what my conflict was. Why couldn't I just tell the truth?

"It's true," I said, and when I opened my mouth to tell Collette the entire truth that she deserved, she fell into my arms in tears. I couldn't tell her yet. I couldn't hurt her more, at least not right now.

During last period, in study hall, I received a text message from Collette. I don't know why I was shocked to receive a text like this from her. Or why I expected her not to go straight to Connor or Theo and confront them. Or why I thought they would let me ruin them without returning the favor.

"Fuck you. I trusted you. You're hateful, and a liar, and I will never forgive you," the text read. I came undone.

I wanted so badly to be angry at Katrina for telling Collette what I had confided. I wanted to yell and scream and tell her how absolutely horrible she was to do that, but she wasn't the problem. I was the problem. I was the core of this entire disaster. The eye of the storm. Connor cheated on Collette but I allowed him to. She was one of my best friends. I should have resisted him and told her as soon as it happened, but I didn't, and now I had to suffer the consequences.

I pulled out a blank piece of paper and a pencil and I wrote a note for my cousin, Camille. She had no part in this, but she was family. I wanted to come clean to her before she heard it from someone else. And while I knew she would disapprove of my actions, I knew she would love me no matter what, and I found comfort in that.

In the letter, I came out to her. I wrote about Connor and the moment when we first figured out our feelings for each other and how it was like a snowball rolling down a hill. How it moved so fast and even though we knew it was wrong we couldn't stop. I told her about Theo and Collette and about every lie I had told over the past year.

I folded the note back and forth over and over until it was a small square and I placed it into my pocket right as the final bell rang. I stood outside of the locker bay waiting for her to pass by. I spotted her with a group of other people and I waved her down.

"Hey, what's up?" She asked. I handed her the note. "Don't read this till you're alone," I said and she nodded. "I love you, okay." I walked away feeling anxious about what was to come in the next two hours of rehearsal with Collette, Connor, and Theo.

I had made a lot of poor choices, yes, but loving Connor was not a choice. There was no help that could be given. I needed him, and there was a time when he needed me too.

When I got to rehearsal and saw that they weren't there, I pulled my phone out and sent him a text message.

"Are you okay?" I asked, but I wasn't holding my breath on getting a response. Still, I kept my phone in my pocket just in case.

Rehearsal was especially tough that day, mostly because of how easy it was. The two hours refused to go by because of how often we would stop so the director could work on a scene that involved only the two leads.

I sat against a wall in the hallway outside of the auditorium and checked my phone. Nothing from Connor. Or Collette. Or Theo. My hands were shaking. What if the three of them had banded together to turn against me. I knew I was in the wrong, but other than Collette, we all screwed up somehow.

Connor cheated on Collette, and Theo and I both let it happen, we both took part in it. In my head, none of us were off the hook...but what if?

"Yeah I heard that Connor cheated on Collette," the words hit me from around the corner.

"I heard it was with Theo!" another voice added.

"No, wait," a third voice chimed in. "I know for a fact that it was Connor and-"

"Connor and who?" I said making myself known to the group of three girls. They looked terrified. Like I had pulled out a knife and was threatening their lives. "No go ahead," I continued. "Say it. Connor and who?"

The blonde girl that I knew only as a freshman working the lighting aspect of the show stuttered trying to find the right words to save herself and her friends.

"That's what I thought," I continued and I must have been angry enough that I was terrifying to them because they all sat there frozen unable to make words. "Maybe mind your own fucking business and don't talk about shit you don't know about."

With my fists clenched, I turned and left rehearsal early without permission. I didn't care enough to stick around. If Collette, Connor, and Theo could get away with not showing up at all, then I didn't care to leave in the middle.

I pulled into the driveway of my home. My hands clasped tight around the steering wheel, my teeth grinding together, my head pounding. I watched my parents through the large window that led into our dining room. My dad sitting at the table typing away on his work computer. My mom on the phone while cooking dinner. They looked so content. I needed to calm down before entering the house as to not disturb their evening.

None of this will matter in just a few years, I told myself. This is just high school. It's nothing compared to the rest of my life. If I could sit there and tell myself that, why couldn't I believe? Why did it feel like my entire world was crumbling around me?

When I got to my room I collapsed into my bed and sunk in under the covers. I thought about an alternate reality where I was like everyone else. The only thing I wanted more than Connor was to not want him at all. To be normal. Then Katrina and I would be together, and I'd be happy with that. I'd come home and talk to my dad about football and to my brother about girls. I wouldn't be lying here in my bed hating every piece of who I was.

My mother called me for dinner. It hurt, but I lazily stood up, changed into sweats, and made my way down the stairs. Maybe it wouldn't be so bad if I missed a step and fell. Hit my head and forgot everything about who I was. Then, maybe I'd find some peace

The next day I scanned the school hallways for Connor. Even though I knew he was upset with me, I still needed to know that he was okay. I stood on my tippy toes in the locker bay looking over crowds of heads until I saw his saggy brown curls, and when he saw me, he immediately turned to walk the opposite way.

"HEY," I yelled catching up to him and then lowering my voice as to make sure no one around us could hear. "You don't get to avoid me. We are all in this."

"We aren't in anything. You told Katrina about me and Theo. I don't owe you anything." His tone was different than I've ever heard it. Harsh.

"The only reason I told her was because I caught you two in the dressing room. I was heartbroken and angry, and you did that on purpose. I could see it in you that you wanted to hurt me."

The crowds in the hallway were thinning. We only had a few minutes before we had to get to class. "You deserved it!" Connor snapped back. "You don't care about me. You slept with him first!"

I was caught off guard. Is that was he thought? That Theo and I slept together? "What? I never slept with Theo...or anyone for that matter. We made out one time and that was only because you and Collette went upstairs together. I was hurt and he was there for me. I only went along with it because I knew you two were going at it upstairs. And then he told me that you have Collette stay the night all the time? Connor, that's frustrating"

The anger left his face, "You two never slept together?"

"No, Connor, we didn't. I haven't slept with anyone," I said. "But you did sleep with Collette. So how am I the only bad guy here?"

He refused to look me in the eyes, even still, like he needed more validation from me.

"Connor," I said. "I care about you more than anything I have ever cared about in my life. You've got me all tied up here. The day that I walked in on you and Theo, I was looking for you to tell you what happened between him and me, and to tell you I wanted things to go back to how they were. I miss you. I'm tired of all the shit."

We stood there the only two left in the hallway. The bell rang but we didn't move. Our eyes locked, and finally, we hugged. Arms wrapped tightly around each other even though we would be marked tardy for homeroom.

"I am so sorry for everything," he said releasing me from his arms.

"I'm sorry too."

"Collette knows everything now, and she isn't so mad at me since I told the truth, but I think she might be out for you."

"It's okay," I said, lying. "I will be okay. I can handle it I think."

"You will be okay. I have to get to class," he said. But before he left he looked around to make sure we were alone, and he kissed me quickly on the cheek.

Connor, I thought, my everything.

A

I was sitting on the edge of the stage, my feet dangling into the pit where the band was practicing. My body swaying dramatically to the drums, making the crowded room laugh.

It had been a week since everyone found out about Connor and me, and for the first time in months, I felt at ease. Like I was my normal happy self again. Connor and I were on good terms, Theo wasn't upset with me at all, and even though I knew Collette might not forgive me ever, I was okay.

It seemed like something like this had to happen to push me out into the open. And if on the way I lost a few friends, I thought I could live with that. That just life, isn't it?

Besides, right now, working on my relationship with Connor was all that mattered to me. We could finally get back to a good place. Where it would be just me and him. No Katrina, no Collette. Just the two of us.

Collette came and sat down next to me, legs crossed, a serious look in her eye.

"Can we talk?" she said, sounding more pleasant than I thought she could ever be to me again.

"Of course?" I said, swinging my legs out of the pit to face her. "What's up?"

She looked nervous now. Like what she had to say would be difficult, and while I waited for her to talk, I mentally prepared myself for the worst.

"I just wanted to say that I am sorry," she said. "While I don't forgive you yet for the things that you have done, I am sorry that you were forced into coming out. I know that must be difficult for you."

I was dumbfounded. Collette deserved an award for her sympathy. Especially since there wasn't even that many people who knew. My secret love affair was known by a select few people in the theatre department who I honestly trusted with my secret.

"Oh," I replied. "Thank you. I appreciate that. I know I really fucked up, but I want to make it right. I can't explain to you how sorry I am for it all. I really felt suffocated, ya know? Like I didn't have any choices even though I did." I took a deep breath. "So, I have to say that I am also sorry…officially."

Collette rested her hand on mine, "It's going to take some time. Not just for you, for Connor too, but I know we will get back to where we were."

I smiled and she pulled her hand away. What I thought would be the worst thing to ever happen to me ended up being the way out of the dark hole I had buried myself in. I had been lying about who I was even before I even knew Connor. Maybe this wasn't what drowning felt like, maybe this is what it felt like to come up for air.

"I am glad we talked," she said.

"Me too."

"Besides," she continued. "Now that Connor and I are officially back together and working on things, we can finally get things back to normal."

My chest caught on fire, and I think she noticed because of the way she shifted her body away from me. "You and Connor are back together as in," I paused for a moment hoping that she would fill in the gap. Instead, she just stared back with a half-smile, knowing that the truth would hurt me and erase the progress we just made. "As in you're friends again?"

"No," she said. "As in we are back together. As a couple."

"Right," I said curtly as I swung my legs back into the pit away from her.

"What is your problem," she said in a yelling whisper as to not call any more attention onto us.

How could she be so naive? How could she think that it would be no big deal? That he would choose her over me, and if he did, that we could all go on as if nothing had ever happened.

"Collette," I stated as plainly as I could. "He's gay. You know this. Why are you digging this hole deeper?"

"He is not gay," she retorted. "He is bisexual."

"Oh, right!"

"He doesn't want to be with you," she said, her voice getting louder. Angrier. "You really need to just get over the idea that you two will ever be together."

I didn't care anymore who was watching or listening. Let them. "How could you possibly think that after all of that he would still want to be with you," I snapped back. The only reason we aren't together is because he was too afraid to break up with you. He didn't think you could handle it, and look at you, he was right."

"So this is all my fault, isn't it?" Collette yelled, grabbing the attention of everyone in the room. Her face red and her hands shaking "You fuck my boyfriend and then make it out to all be my fault?"

I sat there in shock. Unable to move. A claim that wasn't even true, but now everyone, including our theatre teacher, stared at the two of us in the center of the auditorium. The only noise was the buzzing from the stage lights. I felt worn. Exhausted. Collette ran away in tears and it was all my doing. She broke, and it was all my fault.

An hour later and I was sitting in the makeup room. Connor. was sitting across the room in a folding chair. Has hands clasped together, his eyes locked on the floor. The door opened and Collette walked in.

The head of the theatre department locked us in the room so we could talk. "You aren't leaving this room until you can all be civil with each other," she said. "We have a show to put on. We can't be dealing with all of this drama."

"So what," Collette said to break the silence. "We are supposed to just talk it out until we are all buddy-buddy again?" Connor kept still, and for a moment, I even thought he wasn't breathing. Finally, it hit me.

I looked from Connor over to Collette, "The problem is right here," I said gesturing at Connor. "Don't you see it yet?"

The boy who had once been everything I could have ever dreamed of was now the catalyst for all of the hardships in my life. It didn't matter anymore how much I wanted him, I couldn't have him.

"What do you mean," she responded.

"You really can't see it? It's him." I stood and walked towards her. "He is telling me everything that I want to hear and then turning around and doing the same to you."

Connor sat there, still silent, as he knew I was right. Collette pushed passed me and sat in the empty chair next to Connor, "That's not true," she said to me and she forced him to look in her eyes. "That's not true at all."

Connor looked back and forth between the two of us. He was thinking, trying to decide what he wanted. Trying to decide which heart to break and which to preserve. I thought he knew he didn't want to be with Collette, but what if I was wrong? And even if he didn't want to be with her, maybe that didn't automatically mean he wanted to be with me either.

"Connor," I said. "I know you are struggling right now. I am going to make it easy for you."

He looked at my eyes and said my name.

"It's okay," I said. "I understand."

"But..."

"No, it's okay. No more fighting," I started towards the door. "You two have a lot to figure out, but I'm done. I can't keep at this. I'm exhausted. Let's just move on."

Collette had her eyes locked on Connor whose eyes were locked on me. "I wish the best for you two," I said and left them alone together in the room.

Senior prom. The movies always made it seem way more glamorous than it ever was. I didn't want to go only because the only person I wanted to go with was going with Collette. After a long chat with Camille, though, I decided I would go even if it meant I was going alone. If it weren't for Camille I think I would have fallen into my bed and never gotten out of it.

We went as a group. Camille had her date, Tim, and I had mine, Haley. I decided that it would be a good night and there wasn't a thing in the world that would ruin it for me. Mind over matter, I thought, nothing could damage me.

Haley and I entered the ballroom side by side, ready to take on a night full of photographs, good food, and dancing. We took a seat at our assigned table where there were pre-set with plates and glasses and fabric napkins folded into small pyramids that stood on their own. There were even fancy name cards printed on our assigned seats.

Yes, it would be a great night, for sure. Until Haley said innocently, "Oh, look! Connor and Collette are seated next to us!" My heart sank. The universe was playing games with me. I honestly didn't think they would even show up tonight, considering they had isolated themselves the last month and a half since I left them there in that makeup room.

"Yeah," I faked my excitement. "That'll be fun."

"Oh look," she said. "There they are now!"

I looked over my shoulder to see Connor and Collette walking, hand-in-hand towards our assigned table. Collette wearing a gorgeous white and glittery dress to contrast her dark skin and Connor wearing a grey suit with a turquoise tie, which funnily enough, matched what I was wearing better than it matched Collette.

"Hey friends," Collette cheered as they approached the table. "Are we all sitting at the same table? How exciting!" I couldn't tell if she was being serious or sarcastic so I faked a smile just in case. Connor nodded to the two of us. He looked like a model. His suit fit him in all the right ways and if it weren't for the crowded room I could have fallen into his arms right there.

"How have you been," Connor asked smiling at me. "It's been so long." My brain was melting. I suppose I wasn't over Connor like I thought I had been.

"I'm doing well, and yourself?"

"Better now," he said with a smirk, and Collette pretended not to hear him.

Once again, I was nothing but confused. Lost in Connor's web, left alone to figure out whether he wanted to save me or leave me trapped. It was his game, and I had no say in the rules.

Dinner went well. The awkwardness lifted from the air. It

was almost as if nothing had ever happened. Collette and I talked about what colleges we were going to. I was going five hours south to a university in Louisville and she was moving to California for an acting scholarship that she got. Connor chimed in with his plans to go to a trade school and live at home to save money.

It was a perfect dinner with friends. I truly was honestly feeling confident enough to call these people my friends again. When the DJ started up the music we all stood and moved to the dance floor. Over three hundred seniors all in one room dancing the night away to celebrate four long years of high school.

When the first slow song came on, Haley told me she was going to use this opportunity to use the restroom and Collette followed leaving Connor and me alone on the dance floor. I looked at him and smiled.

"What do we do now?" I said.

"Hmm I don't know," he said and then started to sway to the slow love song, around all of the couples that remained on the dance floor. "Let's just keep dancing." I followed his lead and swayed to the music as well.

"I miss you," he said. "I spend all of my free time with Collette but still I think about you every single day." I thought about him too, but should I tell him that? Should I dive back in? I wasn't even sure what he and Collette were. There was no way I could take myself back to where we were months earlier. Sneaking around and lying.

"I miss you too," I said. "But Collette and you...you're together, aren't you?"

"No," he said casually. "We are just friends. Boundaries are set." He had this new confidence in the situation. It didn't seem like he was only there to preserve Collette's feelings anymore.

"Yeah but that doesn't mean she would be okay with you and me being anything more than just friends."

"You're right. I don't think she would like that very much at all."

I stood still and looked Connor in the eyes. Everything I had wanted for so long, since art class two years ago, was standing right in front of me. And for the first time, we were both available. We could do this. Should our mistakes from the past define what we could be today? I didn't think so.

I thought about what our relationship would be like if I had just talked to him in art class or during the summer before Collette and Katrina. What if I had just been brave enough. Not cared what others thought, and trusted that even if he didn't like me back, we could still be friends. Maybe that was the formula to create a working relationship, honestly of course, but also, being brave.

I reached and took his hand in mine. "What're you doing?" He asked with slight panic in his eyes.

"I'm dancing," I said and twirled him around under my arm and back out. He smiled and shook his hips to the beat of the song. When Connor had his hand in mine, nothing else in the room mattered. I didn't care what people might say or think.

And as I danced, I thought, if after everything Connor had gone through over the last year he still would hold my hand and dance with me in front of a hundred other people, well then he must truly want me the way that I have always wanted him. So all I had to do was let myself have it.

Connor and I spent that summer in each other's arms. Our last summer together before I moved five hours away to start a new adventure in college, and we finally had it figured out. No secret love affairs or holding hands under the covers. I loved Connor, and I was no longer afraid to share that with my closest friends.

Camille, Theo, Haley, Tim, Connor, and I spent the long summer days together. Hot days at Camille's Pool. Movie nights in my back yard with a projector that glared at the back wall of my garage. Nights playing ditch in the forest behind Connor's house. We even spent an entire day at the amusement park that was just a few hours' drive away from our hometown.

The five of us hung out in the sun for three months and I had never felt happier or more content in my entire life. But still, there was a shadow looming over us all. Because when it was all over we would all be going our separate ways.

Still, I felt confident about what the future held for Connor and I. Five hours wasn't that long. I could drive home on the weekends and he could even take the bus to come and see me sometimes.

On the last night before we all went our separate ways, the six of us got together for one more bonfire and ditch night at Connor's house. The six of us together to play hide and go seek in the woods, where we had so many wild memories. Like the time Theo fell in the mud and was completely covered from head to toe. Or the time I was lying down and a small snake slithered across my leg sending me into an outrageous panic.

We drew straws to split the six of us into two groups of three. Connor and I weren't on the same team, but it didn't matter to me, because I knew that when the game was over he would still be mine.

My team was the first to hide. While Connors team counted out loud to a hundred I ran to a spot in the woods where Connor and I had spent an evening camping a few months back before everything fell apart. We pitched a tent next to a tree stump and shared a sleeping bag to keep each other warm through the night.

I sat there on the stump and waited, hoping Connor would find his way here. It was a humid evening but the breeze was cold on my cheeks. My heart raced while I waited.

A tap on my shoulder from behind. "Got you," Connor whispered in my ear. I turned and he kissed me on the lips.

"I'm not even mad about it," I responded and we walked back to where we had all started.

We played three more rounds and then settled around the campfire to relax and tell stories. Connor and I sat on a bench and shared a blanket. My hand on his, but now in plain sight for everyone to see.

I stayed with Connor that night. Snuggled up close together in his twin-sized bed. Face to face we didn't have to say a word.

The next morning, I woke up a different person. I had given something that I could never have back. I laid there in that bed, Connor's arms wrapped around me while he slept, the happiest person in the world.

I only had a few hours before I would be packing up my Dad's truck with suitcases of clothing, a new bed set, and boxes of school supplies and books to make the five-hour drive to my new home in Southern Indiana.

I slowly crept up and out of the bed so that I wouldn't wake Connor, but before I got too far his arms reached back around my waist and he pulled me back in. "You don't get to go just yet," he said as he held me tight and kissed my neck.

"I thought you were sleeping!" I said.

"You're not terribly slick," he said and we both laughed.

"I really think we can do this," I said. "I'll come home on the weekends and holidays. And sometimes you can come to visit me if you have a long weekend off."

"Sure," he replied.

"I am finally happy with you," I continued. "It'll be tough but we do this. We can be together." Connor released me from his grip and stared at the ceiling.

"What's wrong?" I asked him.

"It's just that - don't you want to go on this new adventure without anything holding you back? What if you meet someone there? I don't want to be the reason you can't go away and start a new life."

"Connor I don't want a new life. I am perfectly happy with the one I have," I said. He sat up and he looked me in the eyes. I wasn't prepared for what was coming and he knew it. He struggled for a moment. Putting the sentences together in his head as to cause the least amount of damage.

"Look," he said. "You and I have been through so much together. I have known you existed since I was 15, and I have wanted you every day since. I have wanted to love you and I have wanted to hurt you and kiss you and hit you and make love to you. We have all of these nice things that we created together, and they outweigh the not so nice things, they really do. But I don't think those nice things can exist in a world where we aren't even living in the same town."

I was dumbfounded and hurt but still, I fought, "Connor we can Skype every day. I'll call you every night and come home every weekend. We can make it work. I promise."

"You're going to college though!" He said excitedly. "Don't

you want to go and experience that adventure without being tied down?" I sat there silent because that was all I wanted. To tie myself to this bed with Connor so that I wouldn't have to leave everything behind.

"It's not going to work," he said. "I'm sorry."

"You're not even willing to try?" I asked but I already knew his answer. His silence said everything. "So you're just going to sleep with me and then break it off?" He stayed silent while I stood up, the air in the room was cold on my naked body. I picked up my clothes from all corners of the room and started getting dressed. "Fuck you, Connor. You are not the person I thought you were. I regret ever pursuing anything with you in the first place."

I continued to scold him as I put my shoes on. He sat there in silence and let me say my piece. I didn't mean any of it, but my bones were on fire. "I should have told you to fuck off that night you put your hand in mine under the covers. My life would be so much easier without you."

I slammed the door on my way out, hoping that I would wake his parents at this early hour so they would question him.

I hated him, but I didn't. I felt this anger because I loved him so much. I walked home alone and all of those nice things Connor said we had tumbled down and out of me like a raging hail storm.

Later that day, I pulled myself into the back seat of my dad's truck loaded with all the things needed to start this new college life of mine.

I put my headphones in and played a playlist that Connor had made for me almost a full year ago when we were still secretly in love. I rested my head on my pillow against the car door. What was Connor doing right now? Was he thinking about me? Was he cursing himself for not chasing me? Was he content? Not thinking about my heart at all? My heart was hopeful and my brain was sad. The playlist ended, and I fell asleep.

R

I tripped over a loose brick in the patio that my dad and I had laid together as I ran out the back door of my childhood home. My dad and my brother were looking at my brother's car. Heads under the hood, discussing something I could never care to understand. It was not the weekend visit home I was hoping for.

Connor was sitting in his car in my driveway. I needed him, so I called, and he came. Even after I left him naked in his bed months before, he still came through for me.

I caught myself before I completely lost my balance and they both turned towards me. My cheeks were warm and I could feel the water in my eyes. My dad walked up to me and put his hands on my shoulders.

"Hey," he said, trying to get me to look him in the eyes. "Hey, it's okay. It's no big deal. It'll be okay." My mom already told him. Jeez. How did she get to him so fast? She must have called him after I hung up on her.

He was impressively calm. Eye contact. Consideration. Sympathy. He was stronger than my mom was. Stronger than I was.

"I...I've gotta go," I sputtered through my tears. "Connor is waiting for me." He looked concerned but he trusted me. He hugged me tightly. I reciprocated.

"I love you," he said. "No matter what, okay?"

"Okay." I was released and I continued to Connor's car.

"What was that about?" I heard my brother ask my dad as I

slouched into the car. My dad told him it was none of his business. I slammed the car door shut.

"Hey there," Connor greeted me as he pulled back out of my driveway. I didn't respond. My bones were shaking and I couldn't get them to calm. "Hey, are you okay?" I hadn't told him yet why I needed him, just that I did. I texted him and he was at my house within twenty minutes.

"I told my mom that I'm gay," I said. "She knows now and she called my dad and told him before I could." He sat there and drove in silence. It was my biggest fear. He knew how the situation was affecting me. How distraught I was. He knew me better than anyone else.

"Wanna get coffee?" He finally said. "Coffee always makes you feel better." His casual tone gave me a relief no one else could have.

This is not what I wanted. I wanted a casual coming out. Like on TV when two guys kiss in the background and it's no big deal. As if it were a man and a woman. Where the girl brings home her first girlfriend and is welcomed with open arms.

That was how I always imagined it happening. I would bring a guy home - in my mind it was always Connor - and we could sit next to each other and hold hands and kiss each other goodbye. It would be no different than if it were my sister and her boyfriend. Or my brother and his girlfriend. Just two people in love.

Instead, it was an argument over the phone with my mother. Some yelling, a few apologies, and a lot of crying. It was not what I had expected, but it's what I got.

"FINE!" I yelled into the phone, "I'm gay is that what you want to hear? Are you happy?"

I can't even remember what her response was, but I hated

that I was pushed to say it before I was ready to. I still didn't know what it meant, and I still despised myself for it most of the time. How was I supposed to share it with someone else?

I knew my parent's intentions were good. I knew they loved me very much, I just wished they would have let me wait till I was ready.

Connor drove us to a coffee shop a few towns over to avoid running into anyone we knew. He ordered a hot mocha for and a sweet iced coffee for himself and paid. It felt nice to be taken care of. To have every detail thought through to ensure I was comfortable.

He grabbed a deck of cards off the wooden shelf in the back of the room and we sat at a table by a large window. He dealt the cards while I sipped on my hot drink.

"So," he started. "How is college life treating you?" Do I tell him about Chad? How I broke Calvin? Do I tell him that I'm failing my math class? That I'm not getting enough sleep? Do I lie and tell him everything is going really well?

"Everything is going really well."

"That's great to hear!" He said with a smile.

"I want to apologize," I said and his face turned.

"What for?" he asked. My mind raced. For so many things. For hurting him over and over again. For abusing the love that he fully gave me. For leaving him in bed that morning after he said he didn't want to try and make a long-distance relationship work.

"I'm sorry for how I reacted when you said you didn't want to try and make things work," I said. "I realize now they never would have."

"Well I wouldn't say they never would have," he said with a smile and a wink. No matter what he will always make me swoon, always get under my skin.

"It's really okay," he said. "You're always a little emotional." He winked again. Only he could get away with calling me emotional, even though I obviously was.

"Do you want to talk about your parents?" he asked cautiously. His hair was getting longer. I loved it. I loved his brown curls and how he pushed them out of his face when he sipped his iced coffee. He dealt the cards for a game I didn't recognize.

"No," I said. "What're we playing?"

"I honestly don't know," he said. We laughed.

When Connor dropped me off at home, I was relieved to see that no one was there. I sat in the car with him, not wanting to leave. Not wanting my time with him to end. I had to go back to school though.

I had arranged with a guy from one of my English classes to ride with both ways, since he only lived a few towns away from me. He would be at my house to pick me up in less than an hour.

I still had to pack, so I hugged Connor over the center console of his old car, thanked him, and headed inside to get my things together.

The house felt different. It felt bigger. Like it knew what happened and was making room for a new me.

All the secrets and lies were finally out and filling the space. From the bedroom that has been my own since I was twelve, to the kitchen where I used to eat pizza with my siblings, to the living room where my parents surprised us with our first dog on Christmas morning.

All these moments where I was holding something so tightly against me broke away and filled the rooms. I was free.

I felt relief. I felt like I could breathe. Like all of the things that were sitting on my chest evaporated. I knew there was more to come, but it wouldn't be from me holding a secret, it would be from me releasing it. I had stepped into the daylight and let every negative thought from my past run free and far away. My phone buzzed in my pocket. It was a text from Connor.

"It was so good to see you today. I think about you all the time. Let's keep in touch better? Have a safe trip back to school."

I thought to myself, no more lies. This is where life begins.

Mess Me Up

I laid flat on my back in the water, staring at the ceiling of the high school natatorium. What originally I hated, was now my happy place. After months of my fighting my parents about joining the swim team, I finally settled down and into my role on the team. And I was good.

Each day I worked, showed up early to swim extra laps, cardio in the morning, shower, rest, repeat. I swam until my skin absorbed the chlorine and I'd bleed it out into the steamy shower. It was work, yes. Exhausting even, but I wanted to be the best. And since I was only a freshman, I still had three years to get there. Besides that, I enjoyed my alone time. Thirty minutes a day where I was all alone in a deep oasis, and far away from the drama that high school life had brought me. Under the water, I couldn't hear the voices of the other students who bullied me.

All during the school day I would keep my head down. Walk quickly passed the jocks careful not to make any specific eye contact. Straight to class or to the pool to be alone in my head. My free time was mine, and no one would have even thought to disrupt it before Harrison. He was a transfer student who came in at the beginning of second semester. Right in the hectic middle of swim season.

I entered the natatorium early that first day back to school after winter break to find our coach early as well. He stood on the pool deck examining Harrison's glide through the water. He showed off his perfect butterfly stroke and his smooth freestyle technique. I watched in envy as he killed the water with his hands and his body.

"Ah, hey there," my coach said when he saw me, his voice echoing off the walls. "Come over here. I want you to meet someone."

"Okay," I said shyly and watched as Harrison pulled himself out of the water.

"This is Harrison," he said and we shook hands. "He is a transfer student who just tried out for the team, and looks to me he won't have any problem joining in the middle of the season."

"Hey there," he said and he reached his hand out for me to shake. I gave him a brief, but sturdy handshake. Something I had always believed could establish some kind of masculine dominance. My hand shake was stronger than yours, therefore I am stronger than you.

"I think he's going to make a great addition to the team," my coach continued. "He may even find himself on the varsity relay. You're the only other freshman who has been able to achieve that this year."

"That's awesome," I said. "Glad to have you." Even though I felt some sort of competitive jealousy, I would welcome another talented freshman to the team. I knew that in order for *me* to be the best, *we* would have to be the best together as a whole.

That evening at practice, I once again watched him sneak through the water and compared his swimming abilities to mine. We were almost completely equal. He had a hand up in butterfly, but his freestyle couldn't come close to mine. He was muscular enough to pull himself quickly through the water, but I was small enough to glide on top with less effort.

"Okay, everyone," our coach said once we all finished our

laps and were out of the water. "We have our meet tomorrow against South High School." I dried myself off as he talked, barely listening knowing already what events I would be swimming in.

"We have Harrison here who I am going to put into the varsity relay. I want to see how he does in a high pressure situation."

"Wait, seriously?" I said it before I could stop myself, and now I had to finish. "That's...that's my spot."

"I know," he continued. "But Harrison is new and it's not a super important meet, so I'm putting Harrison in it." My cheeks were turning a bright shade of red against the deep blue backdrop of the pool.

"I don't want to step on any toes, Coach," Harrison started. "Maybe I should gain a little seniority before I take someone else's spot. You know, prove myself in practice more?"

"Yeah," I said sounding maybe too excited. "I mean...shouldn't we know how he races before we just throw him in?"

"Well then," Coach started. "Why don't we just have you two race for it right now? First to finish 100 meters freestyle gets to swim in the relay tomorrow."

I thought for a moment, and waited to speak to see if he would first. Maybe, I thought, I should just let him have it. He is new to the team, and Coach was right we should see how he swims under that kind of pressure. The again, I was definitely better at freestyle than he was. I could have this in the bag no problem.

"I'm up for it," Harrison said. "What about you?" He looked at me with a devilish smile. One that said he was ready to take me down, but in a no hard feelings kind of way.

"Let's go," I said already pulling myself out of my warm-up

jacket and walking to the staring block. He followed behind me confidently.

"Okay," Coach said. "Whoever finishes first gets to swim in the varsity relay tomorrow at the meet. No exceptions." The stood in a line against the pool watching intently as we both got into position.

"Ready," Coach said. "Set. GO!" I flung myself from the block and into the water. With streamline precision I pulled my self through the water. Out of the corner of my eye I could see Harrison just slightly behind me, so I pulled harder and faster till he was at least a full body behind me. I came to the wall, flipped, and pushed myself off the wall with my feet which only put me further ahead.

When I turned my head to breath I could hear the team cheering us both on. I reached the next flip turn and did so perfectly. I could see Harrison gaining on me but I knew, still, I knew that I would beat him. I pulled quicker and harder creating waves, and when I came up for the final flip turn, I missed.

I spun my whole body around quickly, but when I went to push off the wall it wasn't there. My feet suspended in open water, and Harrison rocketed ahead of me. I swung my arms around as fast as I could to catch up but the damage was done. When I finally reached the finish line, Harrison was already out and standing on the pool deck.

"Well," Coach said. "Okay well, um, that's never happened to you before...but I guess Harrison is the winner!" I could feel his disappointment in me. It was almost as heavy as my own.

I sat alone in the locker room. Face in my hands, angry at myself for making such a rookie mistake. I had never missed the wall. Never even when I was brand new and barely knew what I was doing.

The locker room door opened and Harrison walked in. I looked away from him to show I didn't want to talk but he sat down next to me anyway.

"Hey," he said. "What're you still doing here?"

"Nothing. I um, I always wait for the other guys to leave before I shower. What're you still doing here?"

"I was talking to Coach about ordering swim suits and warm ups in my new school colors!" He said excitedly. "Why do you wait to shower?" His tone was so innocent and kind. No one on the team ever talked to me like he was.

"It's complicated," I said. "You wouldn't understand."

"Try me!" He suggested, and nudged me with his elbow. I don't know why, but it felt safe to talk to him.

"I don't shower with the other guys because I know that they all think that I am gay, and make fun of me when I'm not around. So I just avoid it all together…it's easier that way for me."

We sat in mutual silence. I thought he was about to stand up and walk away, but instead he said, " Well…are you gay?" I turned to look at him. Shocked, but appreciative. No one had ever asked me so blatantly. People either made heavy assumptions behind my back or made fun of me to my face. Truly, all I even wanted was for someone to simply ask me the question, because no one ever had before.

"Honestly," I said. "I don't know."

"Well that's okay," he said. "Thank you for being honest with me about it."

"Are you?" I asked.

"I am not," he said. "But if you are or aren't, I don't judge you for it. And if you need a friend…I can be that for you."

"I appreciate that," I said. "Seriously more than you know. I'm sorry about being all competitive. But congratulations on winning your spot in the relay."

"Thanks, man," He said. "But really, if you hadn't missed that wall you would have beat me by a long shot. So don't get to down about it…it happens to all of us at some point."

I felt bad for being so rude about the spot in the relay. Harrison was actually very sweet. A kind soul. And someone who could potentially become a very good friend to me. I wished there was a way I could have seen that sooner than I did, and reacted to his presence differently.

The next day at the swim meet I cheered Harrison on in the relay, and he cheered me on in my individual races. The envy that I had felt the day before had evaporated and what replaced it was a feeling of fondness.

On the bus ride home from the meet we sat next to each other in the back and went over our times and tried to come up with ways to improve them.

"I always get to the pool a half hour early so I can get extra laps in," I said. "It's usually my alone time but maybe you could do the same and we could push each other."

"Yeah, I did that at my old school so I'd be down for that."

"Great!" I said. "I really have found that it helps with-"

"Awe look at the two love birds," one of the older guys on the team interrupted. "You two talking about how you can help each other's *stroke?!*" He said, and the whole bus broke out in laughter. I was used to the taunts, and I had gotten used to, and learned how to ignore them. I looked to Harrison, though, and he looked embarrassed. Angry almost. I felt an anxious rise in my stomach. Would he fall in their favor? Or mine?

"Shut up, Jared," Harrison said without even a stutter.

"You're just jealous that you're a junior and the two freshman on the team beat you out for all the varsity relays!" My eyes were wide open. A comment that I thought for sure I'd get a fist to the face for making, but not Harrison. He was emotionally brave, and physically strong. He didn't have to worry about what the other guys would do. He could defend himself.

Jared was shocked, angry even, still he turned around and didn't say another word.

"Thanks," I said quietly, "You don't have to do that. I appreciate it...but you don't have to."

"No thanks required," he said. "You're my friend and I've got your back."

I smiled and we went back to planning our great swimming success plans.

The next day after school let out, I made my way to the natatorium to meet Harrison and get started on our new pre-practice ritual. I turned the hallway into the locker room when I get a text from Harrison, "Hey, I think the schools meaty lunch today made me really sick. I'm headed home right now there is no way I can swim today. Sorry, man. Tomorrow for sure I'll be there!"

I felt slightly bummed by the text, but understood. Harrison was new here. He didn't know yet which lunchroom catastrophes to stay away from. I responded, "No worries. We have all been there. Feel better!"

Maybe one more day to myself in the pool wasn't such a bad thing. It has been a long day and my calculus class has really been kicking my butt lately.

The cold pool consumed my body as I jumped in. The

noise of the day washed off of me, and the sounds muffled by the pressure. The first dive was always exhilarating.

I swam back and forth, back and forth. Removing every mean word said to me that day from my skin and out of my head. I was calm and quick. A delicate brush through the water.

I flipped and turned at the far end of the pool and floated back to the head of the pool, challenging myself. Seeing how far I could get without bringing my face out of the water for a breath. My fingertips grazed the wall and when I lifted my head up to break, a hand grabbed a hold of my hair and shoved me back under.

My arms gripped the wall as I tried to pull myself up but the anonymous hand held me under, pulled me up just for a moment. Just enough for a small unsubstantial breath of air and pushed me back in. My mouth and nose flooded with chemicals in the pool.

When the hand finally let me up I checked and wheezed and struggled to catch my breath. My goggles were filled with tears and my fingernails torn from clawing at the cement wall of the pool. When I came back into myself I looked up to see Jared standing there.

"If you and your friend embarrass me like that again," he said in almost a whisper. "You're going to get a whole lot worse than that." My whole body shook with panic. Caught off guard. I pulled myself out of the pool. My fingers were bloody. I made my way to the locker room pushing passed the other guys on the team as they exited.

"You okay?" my coach asked as he entered the pool room. I couldn't stop crying.

"Yeah," I lied. "I'm fine just have to use the restroom real quick."

The room was empty except for one person. Harrison sitting on a bench near his locker. He looked like he was about to hurl on the floor, and I felt like maybe I could too. I stopped in my tracks when he saw me.

"Hey," he said before really looking at me. "Sorry I missed our pre-workout. I really thought I'd get to just go home but my parents told me I had to be here...oh...oh my god. What happened? Are you okay?"

"I'm fine I just-"

"You are not fine...you are bleeding. What happened?"

I didn't want to tell him. It would only make him angry or feel bad for making the comment he did the day before on the bus. I didn't want him to blame himself for me getting bullied. This was just something that I had gotten used to. Of course it was never physical or potentially life threatening before.

"It was Jared," I said. "He came in early when I was swimming laps and held me under the water."

"Oh my god," Harrison said standing up like his body wasn't completely exhausted from being sick. "I'll beat him. I swear I'll kill him."

He started to move towards the door, but I blocked him with my body, "No Harrison, no. He isn't worth it. Come on just give me a minute to get cleaned up and we can just go to practice. Please, I don't want to make a big deal out of this. I'm used to it...just let it go." It took convincing, but finally he agreed.

I walked to the sink and cleaned the now dry blood from underneath my fingernails and blew my nose while Harrison changed into his swim suit. Together, we entered the natatorium and walked straight to our shared lane in the pool for freshman varsity.

I hoped and I prayed that Harrison wouldn't go rogue and

say or do something to Jared. All I ever wanted was to just keep the peace. I could handle the name calling, and I could handle the occasional shove, but I couldn't handle Harrison getting hurt, especially because of me.

That day after practice I didn't want to go to the locker room, but Harrison convinced me that it would be fine. As always, I sat on the bench in silence to avoid the other guys while they showered before I got in for my own shower. Harrison waited with me.

I truly thought it would be okay. I trusted that Harrison wouldn't cause a scene, mostly because I had asked him not to. And I had hoped that Jared would leave the both of us alone. After such an abrupt encounter, he had to have been done for the day.

In my bloody warm-up suit, I sat in the waiting room at the hospital. My eyes stuck wide open, unable to think or put a clear and concise sentence into any legible structure. My mom sitting beside me almost in tears, trying to get me to tell her what happened. What caused this.

I wished I didn't exist. It's not that I wanted to die, I just wished I never was. Mostly because I wasn't sure what I believed in, and in dying, there could be an afterlife. I didn't even want that. Simply, I didn't want to have ever existed, because it was my fault that I was covered in Harrisons blood. And it was my fault that he was in the hospital.

My coach was at the other end of the room talking to a police officer. Both of them looking at me. I could read his lips that I was a good kid. That I couldn't have had anything to do with this. That "look at him. His eye is black and his nose is still bleeding, there is no way he started this."

The police officer walked towards me and my mother and asked if they could talk to me in private.

"Can I come too?" My mom asked.

"He's under legal age so of course you can. He's not in trouble we just want to know what happened."

We stood and walked with the officer to a room that the hospital had provided to us for privacy. Grey walls with a desk, couch, and a mini fridge.

"Have a seat please," the officer said and my mom and I sat next to each other on the couch. "I just need you to tell me everything you remember about what happened." I looked over to my mom who was almost in tears, and she nodded for me to go ahead and speak.

"I don't know why Jared and Harrison were fighting," I lied. "I just know that it got out of hand really fast. It was like it was nothing and then all at once it was the biggest deal in the world." The officer pulled a chair from the table and sat down, his eyes leaning in on me, telling me to keep going.

"Harrison and I were sitting on a bench in the locker room waiting to take a shower. I think there is more to the story than even I am aware of because it just seems weird that it escalated so quickly. Either way, Jared is a jock. He has friends in every social circle in the school. He came out from the shower and started to taunt us. Just stupid jokes."

I could feel the room shrinking on me. How could I tell the whole truth and also leave out all of the bullying that I have encountered over the past year from Jared? How could I leave out all of the parts about him calling me gay as to not raise suspicions that maybe I actually am.

"And then his friends from the football team came in. It was like he had this whole thing planned to gang up on Harrison. I've only known Harrison for a few days now, but he's a good person. I know he is. Is he okay?"

"I can't talk about his medical record to you...you'll have to wait and talk to him or his parents. Can you tell me what happened next."

"I'd really like to know that he is okay," I begged.

"We can figure that out after you tell me what happened."

I thought back trying to remember every single detail about what happened. About how Jared threw the first punch and how Harrison fought back. How the other guys from the football team ganged up on him.

"Jared and the guys from the football team were all throwing punches at Harrison. Some of the guys from the swim team tried to interfere but there were just too many of them."

"And how did you end up hurt?"

"I tried to get them to stop too. I tried to pull Jared off of Harrison but he elbowed me in the face and then one of the football players held me back. Honestly the fighting wasn't even so bad. Like I said, I don't know Harrison well but I think he could take a few punches without ending up in the hospital."

"His injuries are extremely severe," the police officer said. My hands shook and my head was pounding.

"Yeah I know. Jared got in one good punch that knocked Harrison over. He hit his head. He hit his head really hard on the bench, and then again on the floor, and that's when everyone left. Like they knew this was more serious than a few punches."

The officer sat back and contemplated the story I had told him. It was almost like he didn't believe me. Like He knew there was more to the story. And there was, but it wasn't relevant. It didn't matter that Jared was calling us faggots...it only mattered that Jared did this to Harrison.

"Okay," he said and then he looked down at my shaky hands. "Why are your fingers nails bloody like that?"

"It's nothing," I lied again.

"Please don't lie to me. Why is there blood under your nails?"

"I'm sorry. Before practice I was swimming extra laps and Jared held me under the water. I was clawing at the cement wall to try and get air."

My mom wrapped her arms around me, "Why didn't you tell me this was happening? We could have helped before it got this far." I couldn't make words. I couldn't tell my parents that I was being bullied because then I'd have to tell them why I was being bullied. I'd have to tell them that I might be gay. And how could I confess that when I was still so unsure about it.

"Thank you for your time," the officer said. "You are free to go whenever, but also the room is yours if you need time to relax." He stood and placed a comforting hand on my shoulder. "You may be asked to talk in court if this gets that far. But I am certain you will be okay through it all. Take care, okay?" I nodded and my mother thanked him before he left.

I sat beside Harrison in his hospital bed, tubes connected to each arm and one in his mouth all tangled up and leading to machines beside his bed. His parents told me I could stay as long as I'd like. I was added to the list as a family visitor.

The doctors had run a number of tests and so far everything had checked out okay, but they wouldn't know what his exact state would be until he woke up. They described it as a conclusion that was bad enough put him into a small coma. They felt confident that he would be okay, but it could be days before he woke up.

I had my own injuries looked at and my head checked just in case. Jared's elbow only gave me a small concussion and I wouldn't be allowed to swim for two weeks. Usually that might have killed me but I was happy that I'd have the opportunity to come and see Harrison after school instead of going to swim.

"How is he doing today?" his mom asked me as she walked into the room. It was day two of his coma, and the doctor was predicting about three days. "Sorry I was gone for so long. I needed to get some things at the house taken care of with the other kids."

It was strange to hear about Harrison's life from his mother. I learned that his dad had passed away a few years ago. That he had two younger siblings. His mom worked two full-time jobs just to keep their lives afloat.

"Did he really not tell you about his siblings ever?" She asked me before she left that morning. We sat in waiting room chairs while the doctors ran some more tests on Harrison.

"He was a new friend to me," I said. "We really had only known each other a few days. But we clicked instantly. In a short time he helped me with a lot."

"That's Harrison. Always seeing the good in people and helping to pull it out of them."

"He is doing really well. It's okay. I can stay as long as you'd like me too."

"You're a good friend," she said as she flung her coat over the back of the chair. "I appreciate you being here for him. I know he does too. You're always welcome."

"Mom." Harrison said muffled but he tube hanging from his mouth . His eyes wide open. "Mom?"

"Oh my," she said as she hurried to the side of the bed. "He's waking up! Can you please go get a nurse?"

I stood up fast and ran out of the room to find anyone working that could come and help us. A sea of doctors and nurses rushed into the room and one nurse said I should go wait in the waiting room while they run their tests, and that I could come and see him when things are less hectic.

I sat in the same chair I sat in the first day I got to the hospital. Waiting patiently to hear something. What if he couldn't remember me? They said he could potentially have deficits from the coma. Things like forgetting what happened all the way to losing speech. I was terrified that I could have potentially ruined his life because he stood up for me. His mom exited the room and sat down next to me.

"Is everything okay?" I asked her eagerly.

"I think he is going to be okay," she said almost in tears. "He was asking about you actually. He wanted to know that you were okay after the...incident."

My whole body filled with relief. He was going to be okay. I wasn't going to lose the one potential true friend that I had. I would do anything to make this up to him.

The nurse walked out of the room. "You two can come in now if you'd like," she said. I looked to his mother.

"Go ahead," she said. "I'll come in a few. I think I need a minute alone." I nodded and stood to walk to Harrisons hospital room.

I entered through the wide doorway to see him sitting up in his bed. All the tubes were gone except for one in his arm. He had bed head but still he was smiling.

"Hey there," he said. "How are you feeling?"
"How am I feeling?" I asked. "How are you feeling? You're the one that took a beating!"

"Ah, yeah that is okay though. I don't really remember anything and the pain meds are making me feel pretty good." I sat beside his bed and told him about the police officer, and everything I admitted and everything that I hid. Together, we aligned our stories, and promised to have each other's backs through it all.

"I am so happy you are okay," he told me.

"I am happy you are too," I said. "But seriously...never again."

I Hope You Think Of Me

It had been six months since we broke up, but still every day I thought about the first morning when I woke up beside him. The sun was pushing through his sheer blue curtains onto us lying wrapped around each other on the twin-sized bed in his dorm room.

Perfectly fit together, I laid there in his bed while he slept. His head on my chest, his breathing steady, I tried to match it. I had to drive three hours to my university for a class at noon, but I would lie there for as long as I could get away with before I left.

My relationship with Christopher was complicated and I never thought I'd be the one to end it. After a phone call that lasted 36 minutes exactly, I pulled the plug on a relationship that I thought would be my end game. Christopher was supposed to be the one.

Six whole months passed and still I thought about him every day. Six months and so much had changed. For one, I had moved across the country, from our small town in Ohio to New York. The Big Apple. A whole new shock of culture to take on. It was a job offer that brought me here. It felt like the perfect fresh start after Christopher.

On his birthday, I sat in the middle of Times Square on my lunch break. I stared at my phone with our text conversation open, the last message sent from when we met for coffee to talk about me leaving. I debated whether or not I should say something. I was almost positive if it were my birthday, he would say something.

I locked my phone and put it in my pocket. It was a hot, sunny day in New York considering it was mid-September. One of those days where you leave your apartment in the morning bundled up and by noon you regret that you decided to wear a heavy sweater. The breeze felt nice, though, and honestly the heat was a good excuse to splurge on an iced latte.

When I got back to my office, latte in hand, I felt my phone vibrate in my pocket. A text from Christopher with a photo of us together at a concert. "I miss this," the words read in the grey bubble underneath the photo.

I stood there frozen, between the copy machine and the coffee station, staring at the picture from two years ago on his birthday at the Lana Del Rey concert. The tickets were his gift from me and we spent the evening sprawled on a blanket drinking 20oz beers and taking pictures with my polaroid camera.

I looked at the smiles we had and wanted to not believe them. Moving on would be so much easier, if only I could remember the bad stuff as well as I could remember the good stuff. But it never was that simple was it?

"I miss you too," I typed back and hit send.
Three weeks had gone by and we were talking everyday again. Good morning texts and FaceTime dates during our lunch break. I would tell him how my boss was driving me insane and he would tell me about the dish he was working on in his advanced culinary class.

We reminisced on the good times. When we lived in the same small town and being together was easy. "Remember that time when we were walking up and down the boardwalk?" I asked him.

"Of course I do," He said. "One of my favorite days with you."

It was one of mine too. We walked down a brick path laid down along a lake and picked out pieces of the large homes to create our own dream house.

"I like that one with the wrap around porch on the second story," I said pointing at the house. "But I like the color of that one over there."

"You can have whatever you want," he said. "As long as I get my dream kitchen."

"Okay but can we have dogs too?" I asked knowing how much he hated dogs and that they would always be out of the question. Still, I'd bug him about it till the day I died.

"Sure," he said. "We can get dogs."

"Wait, really?" I asked. He made a move from absolutely no dogs to a casual acceptance of them. "What made you change your mind?"

He took my hand and said, "On my run the other day I saw a couple walking their pack of dogs, and it looked like something I'd love to do with you." I smiled and kissed him on the lips.

"I like you a whole lot you know that?" I said.

"I like you a whole lot too," he said back. "Just no little rat dogs okay?"

The memory sang in my mind. Christopher and I could get back to that. I was only contracted to be in New York for a year and then I could decide if I wanted to stay or go back home. Or even better, Christopher could come here. In a year he would be done with culinary school and New York would be the perfect place for him to dive in.

I was careful, though. I never wanted to say anything to Christopher that might push too hard. That might send him running in the other direction. I was always walking on thin ice, trying to play it cool. A *'yeah I'm cool with wherever this relationship goes'* kind of attitude. But all I wanted was him back in my arms.

"What do you have planned for the rest of the day," he asked me through the screen on my phone.

"I have no real plans as of now, but it's Friday so you never know."

Except I did know. Even though I had been in New York for five full months, I had yet to actually make any real friends. I spent a majority of the time sad over Christopher and the other half trying to make a positive reputation for myself in my work office.

"What about you," I asked.

"I don't have anything I don't think," he said. "But hey I've gotta go. I'll text you later." My phone double beeped and he was gone.

"I need to tell you something," a text from Christopher read on my phone. It had been a week since our last FaceTime call when he abruptly hung up on me.

"Okay," I typed into the keyboard on my phone. "Do you want to call me or?" I hit send and a moment later my phone started to ring. Christopher was the only person in my phone with a special ringtone. The chorus of Made For Each other by Jack's Mannequin filled the room and I slide my thumb across the screen to answer the call.

"Hey what's up?" I said.

"Just sitting in my new apartment," Christopher said, his voice shy. "What about you?"

"Just relaxing at home. My co-workers want me to meet

them out for a drink but I don't know if I want to yet," I said already knowing that I was not even close to considering going out for a few drinks with co-workers. "Wait, you moved?"

Silence. A terrible feeling filled me up, like when Christopher and I had our first fight. I was stressed about one of my school finals. It was an acting challenge and I blamed him for distracting me and somehow a whole world of our rights and wrongs fell from our lips. I yelled that he was afraid of commitment, he said I was too clingy, and the whole thing almost fell apart right then.

To this day I'm not sure how it didn't. He pulled me in and kissed my forehead. I apologized for being emotional and he apologized for being abrasive, and somehow, we made it through. We fought often but we always made it through.

"Yeah, I moved," he said through the phone.

"Well that's a good thing right?"

"Yeah of course it is."

"So why do you sound so nervous, Christopher?" I asked. More silence. "It's okay you can tell me."

"Well the thing is that," he started. "I actually moved in with someone. I've been seeing this guy for a few months now and we know it's really fast but it just feels so right, so we moved in together last week."

I almost dropped my phone. How did I not catch something like this, something so big? How didn't I see that Christopher wasn't only in a relationship, but in one that was serious enough to be moving in with the guy?

"Are you there still?" He asked me.

"Yeah I'm here," I said. "I'm just...I'm just confused." Did I create something in my head that wasn't there? It's certainly possible that this whole time Christopher was happy we were simply just friends again while I was rebuilding our life in my head.

"Why are you confused?" he asked me, which just pissed me off because how could he not know exactly what I was confused about.

"Why didn't you tell me you were seeing anyone? And not only that, but that it was so serious," I was talking faster now. "I truly thought that we were getting back to a good place...that we were-"

"That we were what?" he interrupted me. "That we would get back together?"

"Well...yeah," I stuttered. "I mean yeah maybe, I don't know. I never thought for sure but it was in my head. You put it in my head that we could-"

"I never said anything that could make you think that," he interrupted me again. "You broke up with me, you moved away, you did this to us, remember? I am happy to be friends with you. I actually really want to be friends with you. I love you and I always will. But I will never be in love with you again."

I hung up. Like a child, I couldn't listen anymore. It was an immature move but as he talked at me I could feel the floor falling beneath me in my sixth floor studio apartment. So I hung up. Silenced him. Stopped him from hurting me anymore than he already had.

He was right though, wasn't he? I did this. I ended our relationship and within days picked up and moved across the country. Before I even gave the fiery break-up a moment to settle. I was to blame here, I don't think there was anything I could do to fix it.

The first time Christopher told me he loved me I said it right back to him without hesitation. He was visiting me at my university and I took him to a party at my friend's house. A true college house party with a keg, beer pong competitions, and a DJ.

I asked him to come because I wanted to introduce him to my friends. It felt like an important step. I needed them to see in him what I saw, because I knew that it would still be some time before I could introduce him to my family.

We sat on the couch, his legs over mine, and watched as all the people I went to school with played drinking games. The beer made my head feel hazy and I leaned over to kiss Christopher on the cheek. We had been there for at least four hours now, and I was ready to go back to my apartment so we could spend some time alone before he had to leave in the morning.

"Are you sober enough to drive us home?" I asked him "Yeah," he replied. "I'm good and ready when you are." I rested my head on his shoulder and thanked him.

On our way out the door I listened to echoes of all my closest friends, telling me how happy they were for me. That Christopher was a keeper. That I had found my perfect match. Their words and smiles were honest and excited. I melted in happiness.

Back at my dorm room we laid in my twin sized bed. Twisted together with his head on my chest. I didn't have a roommate that semester so the room was normally lonely. Just me and two closets, two dressers, two night stands, and two twin beds.

He rubbed his hand up and down my back. The room was dimly lit and an indie playlist of songs I'd never heard played softly though my Bluetooth speaker.

"Hey," he said to me quietly.

"Yeah?" I asked.

"You know..." he started but stopped and took a gulp. "You know I love you right?"

I sat up and turned to face him. I couldn't make up a response. Like I knew what the words were but I couldn't find them in the bends of my brain.

"Oh god," he started. "I just totally fucked that up, didn't I? Oh my gosh. I am so stupid it's obviously too soon for that. I didn't mean it...I mean I do but I shouldn't have just blurted it out like th-" I interrupted him with a kiss.

"Hey," I said. "I love you too."

"You do?"

"I do. I'm sorry I just...I wasn't expecting it but yes I love you too. So much."

I kissed him again and he held onto me tightly.

Alone in my apartment, I drank an entire bottle of tequila. It wasn't like me to drink when I was sad, and I didn't mean to do it. But one sip from the bottle turned into a dozen and eventually I was sitting on my coffee table doing back to back shots. A playlist that I created titled "The Great Depression" shot through my sound system.

I picked up my phone and pulled up the text stream between Christopher and I. I looked through all the photos we had sent each other over the years. One of me standing behind him while he washed dishes, my head on his shoulder, both with big smiles. A photo of me from the Lana Del Rey concert holding two 40oz cans of beer. One from our three hour drive from our hometown to his university where I stayed the night before driving another two hours to mine.

All these memories and happy times that used to belong to us, but now belonged to no one. I thought about texting him, stopped myself, and then did it anyway.

"I'm sorry about today," I typed out and as my thumb hovered over the send button and I thought about when Christopher first gave me his number. How I had it for three days before I found the courage to send him a text message. Only because I was nervous that he must have given it to me by mistake.

After all, I was scrawny and awkward, and even though I was only nineteen, my hairline was already starting to recede. Christopher, though, had beautiful long waves and a jawline that could cut. He could have had anyone in the room, so it must have been a mistake that he chose me.

I hit send and poured myself another shot of tequila. This really shouldn't have been so difficult. Six months should be more than enough time to get over a person, right?

"It's okay," his text read across my lock screen. "I understand why you feel the way you do. I feel it sometimes still too. Can I FaceTime you?" I said yes, and within a minute my phone was ringing that same song again.

The world didn't look the way it was supposed to anymore. I slide my finger across the screen and Christopher's face appeared. He looked different. Not happy or sad, maybe it was complacency? Either way, he looked more different than I had ever known him before. And it wasn't a bad thing.

"Hey there," he said through his phones camera and into my living room. I wished he was actually here.

"Hi," I said shyly, trying to hid the fact that I was drunk on tequila.

I could see the blank white walls of his new apartment behind him. A new space for him to settle into with someone other than me.

"So talk to me," he said. "What's actually going on?" I took a deep breath. It was apparent that he still cared for me, and I obviously still cared for him. I supposed I would simply have to adjust my expectations here. Maybe we could just be friends.

"I honestly am okay," I started. "I think it's just this city. I feel suffocated. And I do miss you. Of course I do. And I think I was a little caught off guard by you moving in with someone else so soon, especially since *we* didn't even consider that until we had been dating for almost two years. We were also a lot younger then. I don't know. Work is killing me."

"You're right. We were a lot younger then. We are adults now and everything is different. I think every day about going back. I promise you I do...but it's not real."

"Just because it was my idea to end us...doesn't mean it didn't hurt me just as much as it hurt you," I said.

"I know, I know," he said with a half-smile.

We sat there in silence and for a moment, it didn't feel like anything had changed. Christopher was still Christopher and I was still me. Just grown up. I wanted to make it stop.

I woke the next morning with a booming in my head. Slumped over uncomfortably on the couch. I couldn't remember when I'd fallen asleep. I looked around the room to find it a mess. A half-full bottle of tequila next to an empty one. A storm of papers slung across my coffee table and onto the floor.

When I looked closer, I saw what they were. During the year that Christopher and I lived three hours away from each other, we would send each other handwritten letters. It was Christopher's idea.

"What's your address?" He asked me on a rainy Sunday morning through the FaceTime app on my phone. On

Sundays we would call each other and try to start a movie at the exact same time so it was like we were actually watching it together. "I have something I want to send you."

"I'll text it to you," I said. "What is it?"

"You'll see." I couldn't help but smile. He was always coming up with new ideas to ignite our relationship.

A few days later when I got the handwritten letter, I felt so excited. We would still text and FaceTime every day, but we would also have this third source of communication. We didn't do it all the time. The letters were random and we never knew when we would get one. A way to share the really special thoughts we had.

In my drunken stupor I had pulled the shoebox of letters from under my bed and started going through them. Almost a hundred letters in total, and I kept every single one in perfect condition.

Some of them read happy declarations of love and some told stories of hard days and lonely nights when the pain of being separated was too much.

I remembered some of the letters that I wrote to Christopher myself. The first one where I confessed to being nervous about writing letters and one somewhere in the middle where I finally felt comfortable with the idea.

It was strange at first. Hard to find things to write in a letter that I couldn't just say through a text or phone call...but I remember mostly how it eventually became therapeutic for me. Writing down sentences of love or happiness or anger or frustration helped.

I went to my desk and I pulled out a pen and a piece of loose leaf paper. My head was still pounding and my body ached from all the tequila I had consumed the night before. The sun radiated through the cracks in the blinds and even though I only had an hour before I had to be at work, I sat down and I started to write.

Dear Christopher,

For the last four years you have been my center of gravity. The one to hold me up when everything in my life was crumbling. Like remember that time when I was nervous about my finals and I dropped that plate of food and blamed you? You didn't have the right words but you looked me in the eyes and you held my hand and I felt at ease. I felt brave with you.

I never wanted this to end. The day I met you, I knew that I would want you forever. And even though we grew up and grew apart, still you will always hold the better half of my heart.

There are so many things in this world that I have connected to you. Things that will always make me reminisce on the times when we were happy beside each other. I'll always think of you when I hear that one song about love at first sight and being together forever. I will always think of you when I drive passed that abandoned parking lot on route 6 where we had our first kiss over the center console of my Mom's car.

And when I walk along the boardwalk among all those mansions, I'll think of you then, too. When it's dark and I have a long drive, I'll think of the time when I drove us home from college and you fell asleep with your hand on my leg and how that was the moment I knew I was falling in love with you. I'll think of you when it's rainy and I spend the day in bed binge watching all of our favorite shows.

And when you're feeling sad and he nuzzles his head into your neck, I hope it's me that you think about. Or when you FaceTime during your lunch break because it's too difficult to get through the day without seeing each other. And if it's cold and he gives you his sweater. Or when you're washing the dishes and he hugs you from behind and breaths on the back of your neck and you feel it in your toes. When he sends you random selfies throughout the day. And when you feel yourself falling in love so quickly that time freezes and you feel light as though anything could lift you up, I hope you think of me then too.

And somehow over the years, I hope that we can keep letting go of little things till one day we are both happy and healthy.

All my love X

How To Measure Infinity

I sat squeezed tightly in the back of my aunt's car. Pushed against the door by a pile of sleeping bags, pillows, folded up tents, and coolers full of food and drinks for the long weekend.

I had my journal propped up on my knee, pencil in hand. Trying to write my thoughts but the radio was loud and my head was pounding. It was October but the morning sun was pushing through the window turning the un-airconditioned car into a mobile oven.

"Doing okay back there?" my aunt asked me. My back was covered in sweat but I didn't want to complain.

"Yeah," I said. "How much longer do we have?"

"45 minutes."

I closed my notebook and looked out the window. Stalks of corn blurred as we drove down the empty road. I wished it would start raining.

Every year when the leaves started to change, my aunt and her friends rented a large campground. We would spend four days playing flag football, going fishing, and relaxing around a campfire. The adults spent the weekend drinking and telling stories while the kids roasted marshmallows and told jokes.

One year, the only cousin I have that is close to my age was unable to come. He had a new girlfriend and they were going on a road trip to an amusement park in southern Indiana. Being 18 sounded so much better than being 16.

For me, 16 was a lonely age. I was too young to converse with the adults but too old to run around and play tag with the kids. I was going to spend most of the weekend on my own, and honestly, I didn't mind it. I was good at it.

That year was warmer than previous years. I was wearing a hoodie with shorts and my navy blue Chucks. With dark circles under my eyes, I sat next to the fire pit alone and wrote in my journal.

The sounds of nature were my therapy. Wind blowing leaves, birds chirping, crackling firewood. My home on the outskirts of Chicago was always bustling with noises created by humans, so I enjoyed a break from the city noises.

A grey truck pulled into the campground beside ours. I thought it must be someone from our group that was lost. Normally this time of year we were the only campers in the entire park, but a woman I did not recognize stepped out of the vehicle, and out of the back a little girl with eyes so blue I could see them from my seat across the campground.

I looked back to my journal and crossed out the words I had just written. A notebook full of words scribbled out and written again, and again.

Another car pulled up to the neighboring campground. I could see the silhouette of a person on their phone, gesturing their hands as they talked. The conversation ended and a boy, who looked as young as me, stepped out of the car.

I didn't even know his name, but I remember seeing him and feeling my bones shake. Sometimes I'd see a guy and I didn't know what to name the feeling associated with him. Did I want to be his friend? Did I want to be like him? Or was it something much more delicate?

I watched as he slammed his car door and walked to help the woman, who I decided was his mother, unload the back of the truck. The way his arms flexed when he lifted a bagged tent from the tailgate. The way he laughed when the woman accidentally dropped a 6-pack of beer bottles and they exploded at their feet. How he lifted a heavy cooler from his knees. I was wasted in every move he made.

"What're you doing over here alone?" A voice asked from behind me. My aunt sat down next to me. I closed my journal. "I know it has to be frustrating that your cousin isn't here, but-" her voice trailed off as she noticed the family across the thin wall of trees unpacking their cars.

"That's odd," her thoughts moved from me to the strangers across the way. "We usually have the whole place to ourselves."

"Yeah," I responded, trying to hide my infatuation with our new neighbor.

"He looks like he might be your age! We should invite them to dinner tonight?" Her tone made the sentence a question but she was already up and walking towards them before I could answer.

A few hours later and I finally had my camp set up. I built my tent as far from the rest of the tents as I could. Traditionally, my cousin and I would always share a tent at the edge of the woods. We would stay there and dare each other to stand outside alone in the pitch black for 1, 2, 3, 4, 5 minutes at a time. I decided I would try it by myself this year to prove I was brave enough.

In the middle of the collapsible room, I opened my sleeping bag and made up my bed. It wasn't right the first time so I folded the bag back up and unfolded it again, and then one more time.

Through the white canvas of the room I could make out the blue sky and the orange leaves. There was a cool breeze coming through the netted window and footsteps outside the main door that was held shut by a single zipper.

Slowly, I moved towards the sounds of pacing steps in the yellowing grass of the campground.

"Hello?" A voice came from outside the tent. A deep voice I did not recognize. "Is anyone in there?"

"Uh," I struggled to get up and to the door. "Yeah. One second."

My hand reached for the zipper and pulled it down to open the main door of the tent, and there he was. Wearing a tight black t-shirt with a BAND LOGO I had never heard of and dark blue jeans. I felt my cheeks turn red and when I tried to make words, I couldn't.

"Hi there," he said breaking the silence. "I'm Walter."

"Oh," I replied, hating myself. "Hi."

I unzipped the door the rest of the way, climbed out of the tent, and zipped it back up behind me. Then unzipped it, then back again. I caught his confused look as I unzipped and zipped it back up one more time.

"Sorry," I said. "I have to do it."

"It's cool, man. No worries." His mouth was smiling but his eyes were concerned. I reached my hand out to shake his and we properly introduced ourselves. He was here with his parents and sister for the weekend. They did this every fall, just like us, but normally they came a month earlier. He told me this was the only weekend with open slots.

"So, it was your aunt, I think," I loved the way he talked with his hands, "she invited us to have dinner with your group tonight."

"Yeah, she told me. Are you going to?"

He nodded, "Yeah I think so. My parents ran to the grocery store a few miles away to get something to bring. My mom told me I should come introduce myself to you...so here I am."

"That's cool, man." I was trying too hard. He could see through me. "What're you up to now? I was thinking about going on a walk before I have to be back to help my aunt."

"Yeah, sure. A walk sounds nice."

With him beside me, I walked together along a man-made trail in the woods about a mile to a waterfall that I knew of. Previous years I'd go there when I needed some time to myself, which was often. I never took anyone there until that day.

We sat on a fallen tree and watched the water flow and fall down the side of the hill and into the river. We learned about each other. He was 17 and he went to a high school a few cities away from mine. He was on the soccer team and loved to write.

"People always give me weird looks when I say my dream is to publish a book," he said. "I guess if you're a jock that's all you can be." I understood him. I wasn't nearly a jock, and while I loved to write fiction, I was more of a poet than anything else. I understood in a different way. Once a person sees me wash my hands six times or opening and closing a door three times before entering the room, that's all they see.

"I know what you mean," I said pulling at the cuff of my shorts with my left hand. I hoped and hoped he wouldn't notice. We sat in silence.

"Do you always do that?" He asked me.

"What?"

"You know, that with your hands. Do you always do that or are you just nervous right now?"

No one had ever so boldly asked me about my tendencies.

Usually, people noticed and then tried forever to avoid it. Like I'd fall apart if they interrupted me in the middle of a tick.

He placed his right hand on top of my left and held it still. My chest was beating quickly, loudly, painful almost. I had never tested the waters of what might happen if I was forced to stop, and it felt like I was losing air.

"Hey, it's okay." He assured me, "Just take a deep breath. Slowly."

I didn't think a deep breath would help, but it did. I took another. And another and the world came back into focus.

"Have you always had this happen?" He asked pulling his hand away. I wanted to grab it back and tie it to mine.

"No," I responded. "Well kind of, but they only got really bad in the last year and a half."

"Why do you think?"

"Um," I was stuck on how honest I should be with someone I had just met. I barely talked to anyone about it, except for my therapist.

"You don't have to answer that if it's too straightforward," he added seeing how flustered I was.

"It is," I said, "but it's okay."

I took another deep breath. He watched as I pulled at my shirt and he smiled. It put me at ease. I don't know how or why, but I felt comfortable. My mind was constantly running at hyper speed, but around him, I could slow it down. I sat on my hands, took another heavy breath and told him my story.

"Almost two years ago I was in a car accident," I explained. "My older brother was driving and we were hit by a semi-truck. I don't remember a lot, but I do remember yelling at him to stop because he was texting and the light we were coming to was red." His face changed from a small smile to straight.

"I think that when I yelled at him to stop, he panicked and accidentally hit the gas pedal instead of the break. So we ran the light and got t-boned by another car. I woke up a few days later in the hospital, and when I found out he didn't survive, I fell into something." I pushed my hair out of my face three times and placed my hand back under my leg.

"My therapist says that my brain was just too young to cope with something so big and now I have these 'ticks', as he likes to call them. It's a way your brain deals with trauma. Like it's sending the stress to other parts of your body so that it doesn't have to think about it." I pulled my hands from under me again and adjusted my shirt. "He says I'll grow out of it, but two years later and it seems like it's always getting worse. New things are always coming up."

He rested his hand on mine again. This time, not to stop me, but to tell me that it was okay.

I sat down on a bench in front of the fire pit with a bowl of chili and propped my leg up to save him a seat next to me. I wasn't sure what was going on in his head, but I knew that somehow he calmed me. I was comfortable with him. I liked him.

The sun was setting and the sky was on fire to match the leaves on the trees. I admired all the different colors in the sky and how they faded into each other so seamlessly.

"Here ya go," Walter said sitting down next to me. He was holding out a plastic cup full of red Kool-Aid.

"Thank you," I said smiling. "Are you not eating anything?" He was holding a cup just like mine but no bowl of chili.

"Not right now," he said and took a sip of his drink.

I took a sip from my own cup and choked on the taste. I

had never tasted alcohol, but I knew what it smelled like, and it tasted how it smelled.

"Walter!" I halfway shouted, "This has alcohol!"

"Shhh! Do you want to get in trouble?"

I didn't want to drink it, but I didn't want to accidentally tell on him either. So, I turned my voice into a whisper.

"I don't care if you want to drink but I can't," I said. "I don't want to get in trouble."

"They'll never know…they've been drinking all day!"

He was right. My aunt and all of the other adults had been drinking since we got there that morning. I thought for a moment and took another tentative sip. It wasn't so bad since I knew it was coming.

"Okay but just this one," I said as sternly as I could.

"What?" He rebelled. "You do everything else in three's and six's but you'll only have one drink?" I looked into his eyes. I wasn't sure yet if I was okay with him joking like that. I wanted to be okay with it. I wanted to be able to laugh at his jokes that poked fun at my trauma.

Walter lifted his cup and took another sip. "Come on," he said. "It won't be a big deal. Loosen up a little." He ran his fingers through his hair and gave me a subtle wink. I was captured by him. So I chugged my own drink and then asked him to make me another.

The trees were spinning around me as I walked back to my tent. Cursing at myself for building my fort so far from everyone else. One drink turned into five and even though it made my brain twist, I couldn't bring myself to have a sixth.

Walter was barely phased. Or I was so phased that in comparison that it seemed like he wasn't. I stumbled my way across the open campground and about halfway to my tent I decided to take a break and lie down.

The grass tickled the back of my neck but I didn't mind because I could see every star in the sky. In the city, you're lucky to see a few stars. Here in the middle of nowhere, you can see thousands.

I thought about space and infinity. How I wish I had a way to measure and understand it. How can a human measure infinity? I tried to come up with something but the alcohol refused to let me think right.

"Whatcha doin'?" Walter asked funnily as he laid down beside me.

"Thinking."

"Thinking about what?"

"Space."

He turned his head towards me and then back up at the sky and then back at me again. I could feel his eyes on me. They were pulling at me, begging me to turn and put my eyes on him.

"What are you thinking about now?" He asked.

"You," I admitted. "You. You." Three times.

"I think about you too."

I turned my head towards him. He moved closer to me and put his lips on mine. Quick. Simple. Like we had done it many times before.

In my tent, I pulled his shirt over his head and kissed and kissed and kissed his neck. He moaned my name and I kissed him on the lips. His eyes opened up into mine and he held my hand.

"Can I?" he asked me. I nodded.

"Go slow." I had been terrified of this moment, but with

Walter I felt calm. He held my hand and my body relaxed. That was exactly where I was supposed to be. Exactly where it was supposed to happen.

It was quick but I remember every moment. How he kissed me passionately. How it hurt in a way I had never experienced. The pressure, then eventually, the immense pleasure.

This, I thought, *is how you measure infinity.*

He used his t-shirt to clean the mess he made on my smooth chest, then laid beside me. A heavy sigh. A hand on my hand.

I thought about whether or not I should say something. Ask him if he is okay? Ask him to do it again? If I was his first? Tell him he was my first? My head was still spinning from the alcohol.

"Wow," I said finally.

"Yeah." He giggled and then I did too.

"How," I paused and thought of how to phrase what I wanted to ask. "How long have you known?" I had never had a person in my life who I could talk to about liking guys. I think I knew my whole life that I did, but never knew exactly what it meant.

"Know what?"

"That you're...you know..." I was careful not to use the word.

"That I'm what?"

"That you like guys..."

"Oh," he said flippantly. "I don't."

I was confused. How could he be so casual?

"But you..." I started, "it's okay if-"

"I'm not into guys, okay?" His voice was angry now.

He sat up and started getting dressed. No words. His movements were quick. His face twisted in anger, or embarrassment, or regret, or a combination of all of it.

"Walter, I'm sorry I didn't-"

"I'm not a faggot," he interrupted me again. I wasn't sure how to respond. I understood his pain but I didn't know how to make it stop and I didn't know how to make him stay. He pulled his dirty shirt over his head and down his body.

"Wait...I,"

"You what?" His voice was harsh. His eyes dark in the night. He started to unzip the tents only exit. I wanted to fight for him to stay. I wanted to beg him to stay, to talk to me. To apologize to him. To make it right. To understand him.

I laid my hand on his shoulder and he turned around and hit me in the face. "Leave me alone," he said, and then he was gone.

I laid my head down the pillow. You could see the stars through the roof of the tent and I cursed them. I didn't believe in God, but still, I prayed for Walter to come back. I prayed for him to come and hold me in his arms all night and make love to me again when the sun came up.

I sat up to close the opening in the tent Walter had left out of. I zipped it shut, then opened it up. Zipped it shut, then opened it back up. One more time.

I finally felt tired when the sun was coming up. Peaking over the forest and into my fort. My body was sore. I felt like I could throw up. I wanted to throw up. Rid myself of the poison I consumed the night before along with all of my memories of the night.

I wanted to hate Walter, but I understood him too well. I wanted to go find him so we could talk about what happened. Maybe he was feeling as pained as I was.

It was almost 6 am. I crawled to the tent door and exited. I stood and turned to do my normal open and close routine. Instead, I threw up, and my stomach felt better.

I slipped into my hoodie, pulled my shoes on, peed on a tree behind my tent, and then started walking towards the trail that lead to the waterfall. I had a feeling that was pulling me there. He knew that's where I went so maybe that's where he would go too if he wanted to talk.

He wasn't there, but still, I was happy to be there. Alone with my thoughts. I dipped my hands in the water and rubbed my face. My first hangover and it was a killer. The cold water eased my pounding head.

I thought about the passionate moment Walter and I had. Is this what it would always be like? Did me being attracted to men put me into a category that doomed me to constant heartache?

When I got back to the main campground my aunt was up with Walter's mother making mimosas for breakfast. They looked as sick as I did, but my aunt always said the best cure for a hangover was to drink more.

"Hey Hon," my aunt said. "I didn't realize you were up and out already."

"Yeah," I responded and pulled at the strings on my hoodie." I didn't get much sleep and a walk sounded nice."

"What happened to your eye?" She asked. I brought my fingers to my face and felt the swollen skin.

"Oh," I had to think quick. I couldn't tell my eye was swollen and bruised because of Walter and everything that had happened. "I fell on my way back to the tent last night when it was dark."

They sipped their mimosas and sat next to the burned out fire pit. My aunt waved at me to come sit and hang out. I took a step forward and then back.

"Actually," I looked at Walter's mom. "Is Walter awake yet? We were supposed to go fishing today."

"Oh no I'm sorry," she said. "He wasn't feeling well and decided to drive back home this morning."

It took everything in me to not show them how broken I was. My face was warm and there was a crying pressure in my eyes.

"Oh," I said. "You don't think he'll come back?"

"I doubt it. He really didn't look good when we talked."

I nodded and faked a smile.

Two days later and it was time to go home. I was, once again, crammed uncomfortably in the back seat of the hot car. I pulled out my journal and looked over everything I had written and scribbled since the morning after Walter.

I used up all the pages with poems about my first time and the twist in my stomach I felt because of it. Poems about the first taste of alcohol and the way it made my head dizzy. Poems about how Walter held my hand and comforted me when I needed him to. Poems about how when I asked him to stop but he didn't. About the emotional marks he left on me, and about the physical ones too.

Once again, the stalks of corn blurred passed the car window, and finally, it started to rain.

Last October Fifth

"I wish I'd told you the truth," I whispered. "I wish I could go back." I stood from where I'd been sitting beside the hospital bed and walked to meet my parents in the cafeteria. We all knew it was coming, but I always thought I'd have more time.

"You okay?" My dad asked me.

"Yeah," I said. "I just don't want to be here anymore. Can I go home?"

"Yeah, I'll let you know if there are any changes." We hugged and I walk through the automatic rotating doors of the hospital and out to my rental car.

Coming home to visit was always exhausting. Buses, trains, planes, and car rides always wore me out. This time was circumstantially different though. There wasn't a wedding or birthday party. It was the complete opposite.

I drove home and changed into sweats and a hoodie. I had the whole house to myself. I went to my voicemails from last October fifth and found the one from my grandma. Every year on my birthday she would call and sing happy birthday, but you had to let it go to voicemail. One year I made the mistake of answering the call.

"You're not supposed to answer!" She yelled at me with her little voice through the phone.

"Oh," I said. "Sorry, grandma! Redo!"

A moment later my phone started ringing again and I let it go to voicemail. I imagined her sitting at her chair in the kitchen, singing quietly so no one around could hear her and then searching the phone for the button to hang-up.

I sat on the couch and listened to her sing to me. The happiness in her singing, and the pride she felt when she finished and yelled "Happy Birthday, hun!" It was all a heavy contrast to where she was now. Lying in a hospital bed with tubes in her arms.

I always knew this day would come, but it always felt further away than this.

A few days later my cousins, siblings, and I sat in a circle in the living room where we had celebrated so many Christmases, and Thanksgivings, where we stopped by to show off our Halloween costumes and snag king size chocolate bars. Photos from shoeboxes were scattered across the floor.

I picked up a Polaroid photograph. I remembered the day so well. My little cousin had gotten an old Polaroid camera that Christmas and he was so excited to be running around taking pictures of everyone during our Christmas dinner at my grandmother's house.

The bottom of the photo read "2011" in bold Sharpie marker. It was the year I had gotten my own cell phone. In the picture I'm sitting next to my grandma at the kitchen table, her cutting up potatoes, me playing on my new device.

"So are you going to spend the rest of your life looking at that thing, then?" she asked me right after the snap was taken.

"I don't know, maybe!" I said laughing. I put the phone back into my pocket. "Sorry, can I help you with anything?"

"He's texting all his girlfriends, I'm sure," my aunt chimed in jokingly. "All the girls must want you, being the swim star that you are!"

In these moments I used to panic. My mouth would dry

and I wouldn't know what to say. How to hide the facts about who I was from the people that I loved.

"Are you still dating that one girl? What was her name? Started with a 'K' I think," my aunt added.

"No, we aren't," I said. "I'm not dating anyone. I don't want to be."

I had lied so much that it didn't even feel like a lie. Small lies. Tiny enough that they really didn't even matter. The truth was that I was seeing someone. But it wasn't a girl at all. I was in love with a boy, and not a single person could know that.

"Smart boy," my grandma said not looking up from the delicate cutting work she was doing. "You can date when you're in college."

Thinking back now the lies felt so easy to tell, but they were only pushing me into a pile of shame. A little bit piled on at a time. Slow enough that I didn't even notice at first. Like it was normal to lie to the people you loved about who you were. To lie to the people you loved about how you loved.

"Can I keep this Polaroid?" I asked my aunt, who had deemed herself in charge of the photo boards for the funeral. "I know it looks dumb 'cause I'm on my phone, but I just remember that moment so clearly."

"Of course you can," she said. "You can keep any of the photos you find that you're in with her."

I took the Polaroid and placed it gently in my backpack, "I think I am going to head home," I said. "I am feeling a little overwhelmed."

Two days later at the funeral home, I hovered in the back of the room, avoiding making my way to the front where she was. I felt shame, and I didn't deserve to be at rest until I found a way to come clean. To wash all the lies away.

I thought about the last time I was in that funeral home. It was at the wake for one of my dad's friends who he grew up with. I sat next to my grandma while she told a story about my dad and his friend getting into all sorts of trouble when they were young kids.

I remember placing my hand on her back to comfort her when she started to cry, and I wished that she was beside me now to comfort me. To tell me everything was going to be okay.

My mom came up beside me and said she would walk up to the front with me if I needed. That this was the last day I'd have to get to see her, so I needed to do it even if it was difficult. "She loved you," my mom said. "She loved you so much. You need to go say goodbye to her."

Slowly, I made my way to the front of the room. Passed all of the photo boards that we had meticulously pinned together over the two days before. Passed all of the wreathes and bouquets of flowers from friends and family and old co-workers.

I stood next to the casket. I wasn't sure what this was supposed to do for me. We have created all of these traditions that are meant to help you cope with death, but I felt nothing.

I drove alone down the curvy road of the cemetery. The only noise came from the worn out windshield wipers squeaking as the swayed back and forth across the window. Three days had passed since the funeral, and like out of a sad movie, it hadn't stopped raining.

I pulled over in the same spot that I had three days earlier when we lowered the casket into the ground. A pile of dirt the only indicator of where we all gathered around to watch.

My mom told me it might be hard to find. That the headstone wouldn't be installed for at least another few weeks while it was being engraved. Still, I found I needed to come and say something. Anything.

The small umbrella barely kept me dry and my socks and shoes were already soaked through after only a minute outside. I kneeled in the mud and placed a bouquet of flowers on top of the pile of dirt.

I thought I would come here and see what felt right. Should I talk? Or sit in silence? Wait for a miracle? For a moment, I felt stupid. What about this was going to help me? How was this grieving?

"Hi Grandma," I said out loud. The light rain drops splashed around me and I fought to find the courage to say more. "It's me. You know who I am."

The more I talked the easier it got, "I don't know what I believe in. I don't know if you can hear me or see me or if at this point you are just completely gone or if you're...all knowing or something." I looked around to make sure no one else was around before I continued.

"Well, anyway...I just came here today because I wanted to say that I'm sorry. For so many different things. For lying to you for so long about who I am and what I have been up to. I know you wouldn't be proud of all the lies I've told over the years, but I know you still love me no matter what.

"I guess I just needed to tell you that I like guys...well, and girls sometimes. People, really. I like people. Romantically, I like people. And while I have worked hard and found comfort and confidence in this, I do not feel good about having lied about it for so long. Or maybe you always knew and were waiting for me to say something? Or maybe it never really mattered to you? I...um, I just needed to let you hear it from me." The rain was starting to let up.

"I've have always kind of prided myself on not needing to have some big coming out. I never wanted to make every part of me about this one thing. But recently, I've realized how important it is. Because this is a part of the way that I love people. And that part of me is important. That part of all of us is important."

I closed my eyes for a moment and let myself cry. I wanted to make sure there wasn't anything else, but I couldn't find anything. A weight had been lifted off of me, and the tears felt freeing.

I stood and walked back to my car, covered in mud and my clothes soaked, I was at ease.

That's Not What I Meant

When you're a kid, you sometimes don't understand that jokes are just jokes, and that's what I was trying to explain. When you're thirteen years old and already confused about who you are, it's hard to take things not so seriously, was my point.

Still, he kept going. His voice getting louder. Drawing more and more attention from the other partygoers. A small anxiety growing in the pit of my stomach and getting bigger with every breath I took, every time I tried to speak but was interrupted. Every time he raised his voice a little louder.

This situation was one I had played over and over again in my head for years. On long car rides and in lukewarm showers, I pictured what this moment would look like and what I would say and the points I would make to defend myself.

"I just don't know why you couldn't tell us you were gay sooner," he said. "You lied to us for all these years. You didn't trust that we would accept you."

"It's hard to explain," I retorted. "I can't explain what it feels like when you're a child and you hear the adults in your family making jokes about the gay neighbors or the lesbian at the bar. I didn't understand then that they were jokes. When you're a little kid it feels like attacks."

"So you're just going to blame all of us. Your family. As if this isn't completely your own doing?"

The whole thing came about because my cousin, Greg, asked me if the word "faggot" offended me. I was caught off guard but happy to answer. He legitimately wanted to learn and understand.

I explained to him that, personally, I knew what he meant when he said it. That I wasn't offended, because I know and love him, but to consider the history of the word and what it might mean to someone who didn't know him at all.

It was funny really, only because I never actually came out to my family. I had told my siblings and my parents a few years before, but never felt ready to tell my extended family. Though, somehow, everyone knew and it was okay, and I didn't need to say anything. It felt almost pretentious to me to have a huge coming out. If they asked me, I'd be honest, but other than that, I didn't want to draw attention to it. It's not like my siblings had to come out as straight, why should I have to come out as gay?

"I didn't do anything to myself," I tried to explain. "And you didn't do anything to me either. I just needed to come to terms on my own time." I felt mostly calm but also my hands were starting to shake.

"You didn't even give us a chance. You just lied and lied and lied."

"You don't get it though," I said. "You'll never understand what it's like to be minority, especially in a family like this whose-"

"A family like this?" he interrupted me, obviously offended even though I didn't actually get to finish my sentence.

"…A family like this, full of straight men who were all top-class athletes."

"So then it's my fault for being good at sports in high school?" He asked in an obviously rhetorical way.

"No, that's not what I mean I'm just saying no one did anything wrong but the circumstances made things more-"

"I don't even care to hear this," he said.

I took a moment to think about how I should handle this situation. At this point we had both said things. We had both been rude. We had both been offensive in different ways. Maybe he called me a liar and a joke but I had my words too.

But while I sat there silently, and he kept yelling, getting louder and louder, my walls were slowly weakening and I felt like I was in middle school again. A terrified skinny little boy who nobody liked. Who people made fun of because of the way his voice sounded or the way he walked. How guys would accuse me of looking at them in the locker room and push me down and kick me in the gut to teach me a lesson. And I gave up.

I was done. I said I wasn't here for this anymore, and I walked away. Through the crowds of my large family that stood by and said nothing while he tore me to shreds. Took something from me that I had worked so hard to get. My confidence, my happiness, my comfortability in my skin. The feeling like who I loved didn't matter. Like I could finally be free in front of my family. It was all gone.

Before I knew it I was sitting on the couch in the living room, crying, sobbing, unable to breath, because of it all. Pulled apart by someone who ultimately didn't matter to me, and I knew that, but I couldn't stop.

My dad came in, not knowing what had happened and when he saw me, sat down and pulled me in. I didn't know what to say other than 'I'm sorry' over and over again.

"What are you sorry for?" He asked.

"For lying to you for so long."

"What're you talking about?"

"We were out by the pool talking and Jay started yelling at me about how I was lying to everyone for so long about being gay."

There was a moment of silence because my cousin Camille came in and also asked what happened. I explained and I think if it weren't for my dad being so calm, she might have gone and murdered Jay.

"Son, you never lied to any of us," my dad said. "We all know that. You were just protecting yourself. You had no way of knowing how we would react, and no one blames you for keeping it to yourself for as long as you did." He had the exact words I needed to hear, but still I wanted to just go home. I didn't feel comfortable. As much as I wanted to belong here, I didn't feel like I did.

The next day I sat at my desk to work but my writing could not keep my focus. My editor was on me about a deadline that was quickly approaching. "You know this is being posted tomorrow morning, right?" she asked me. "You have yet to send me any drafts. That's very unlike you."

Even though my head was full, I guess my creativity was running on low. I had only been working for this online publication for a few months, but I took a liking to it quickly. I used to write exclusively journalistic style pieces. Now I wrote fiction, and the creativity of it brought me a new joy.

"I'm working on it, I promise." I told her through the phone. "I'll have it to you in the next few hours."

"I sure hope you're right," she exclaimed and then wished me good luck.

I stared at my screen. Half of the story was already written. I just needed to find the way to end it. The night before at the party still consumed my mind. I couldn't understand why this really took ahold of me. Why did I care so much about the opinions of these people? I knew who I was, and I knew my character. So why did I care?

I pulled my phone out of my pocket and called my mom. No answer. I figured she must still be sleeping but then I got a text.

"Sorry, I can't talk right now. Is everything okay?" It read.

"Yeah. Just a little stressed...wanted to chat."

"Because of last night?"

"Yeah, can't think of anything but that..."

"Why don't you write about it then? Just vent about it and throw it away. Like you used to do in your notebooks." She suggested, and I took a moment to consider it.

"Good idea!" I typed back. "I'll try that."

I placed my phone in my bag so that it would no longer be a distraction. It took me a minute to figure out exactly where to start with it, but once I opened the new document on my computer, my feelings took over.

I smeared all of the emotions I'd had since I was a little kid onto a page. About growing up gay in a small town. About having a family that most likely would be supportive, but to know for sure could be catastrophic. The constant lying and sneaking around that came with it as well. And before I knew it, I had a 5,000-word document displayed in front of me.

As always, my mother was right. I did feel better. My head felt clear. Getting the feelings I was having out of my head and into sentences was the perfect way to sweep the whole thing off my back and into the past.

I closed the document and pulled up the story that I had been working on for two weeks now. A short story about two lovers being pulled apart and pushed back together over the span of five years until they eventually end up together and happy and living in Manhattan.

Slowly, I pulled out another sentence, that led to another paragraph, and another. And within just an hour, I had a finished story. I pulled my phone out and texted my editor, "Sending you the finished document now."

I logged into my email and dragged the saved document from my desktop with today's date into the email, let it load, and hit send. The clock on my desk told me that it was half past five. It was time to head home and not think about work for the rest of the evening.

I felt good about this story. It was so different than the other ones I had written since writing fiction. I left the office thinking that maybe this one would be my big hit.

When I got home I put on some trash television and opened a bottle of wine. My phone chimed in my bag, and I considered not checking the email, but decided to just in case there was an issue with the article.

I swiped my thumb up to unlock the device and opened the email from my editor.

"This is not the story I thought you were writing but I love this so much better. So raw and emotional and REAL! Congrats on this! We are making it the headliner for tomorrow's online release!!!"

My whole body was tense. I should have felt excited, but something felt off. I had a good feeling about this story, but to call it "raw" and "emotional" felt a little bit dramatic. I pulled out my laptop and went to my sent emails, found the one with from just an hour ago, and opened up the document.

My heart stopped. I had sent the wrong one.

The next morning my alarm went off at seven am exactly, but I was already awake. After a half hour long phone call with my editor begging her not to post that story, exclaiming that it was a mistake, and making empty promises that the one I meant to send was much better, I gave up.

All night I tossed and turned. What would this mistake lead to? My personal life was about to become a banner in New York City, and my whole family was going to see it. All the lies I've told, and the hardships I've overcome, all of the terrible mistakes I've made.

I peeled myself out of the bed and avoided turning my phone on. Took a long hot shower, and made my way out the door to walk the seven blocks to my office.

In the elevator, I finally found the courage to turn my phone on. I was expecting to have an explosion of texts and missed calls from my mom or maybe my cousin. But there was nothing. Maybe everyone was too mad to even yell.

I stepped off the elevator and into the office to find all of my co-workers, smiling, gathered around, clapping, cheering to me. My editor wrapper her arm around me and gave me a big hug. I must have been dreaming, I thought.

"Okay…What's going on?" I asked.

"You haven't heard yet," She said. "Did you not get my email this morning?"

"Oh no, I haven't checked it yet," I said almost annoyed. "What's going on?"

She put her arm back around me and turned me to face all of my peers. "We all want to congratulate you on your story! It posted this morning and in only three hours, it is our most shared and highly reviewed story yet! You're trending!"

My face was warm. I felt like crying, either from joy or an overwhelming sadness. There was no way my family wouldn't see the article if it was this big of a deal, but also this kind of a success could mean so much for me.

I smiled and my eyes watered at the same time and it felt good and it felt scary. My phone vibrated in my pocket and I pulled it out to see a text notification from my mother. I unlocked the screen to see the message read, "Okay well...that's not what I meant."

Help Me Hold Onto You

He grabbed my hand and pulled me forward through the crowd of inebriated men. I didn't love to dance, but for him, I'd have agreed to do anything. We found a spot in the middle of the dance floor and I watched as he clumsily swung his arms around in the air.

I took a deep breath and slowly swayed, while I found the courage to join him. We had only known each other for a week, yet I felt more comfortable with him than I did alone with myself.

A remix of Whitney Houston's I Wanna Dance With Somebody shot through the speakers and shook the floor underneath us as we danced as hard as we could. His sweaty body against mine, his hands on my hips.

There was a feeling I hadn't experienced in so long that I wasn't sure what to call it. I felt excited and happy. Solid and healthy. I tried to keep my cool but he could see right through me. I just knew it.

I could feel myself breaking open for him. Tearing me apart from the insides and putting me back together. Because I did not do this. I did not easily open up. With him though, I wanted to share all of my best and worst times.

He pulled me close and put his lips to my ear, "Wanna get out of here?" I looked him in the eyes and nodded.

That night I slept beside him. On my side with my arm draped over his waist and his fingers locked in on mine. A rotating fan the only noise in the room. His queen-sized bed just small enough to hold us close together.

When the sun came up and pushed through the window above his bed I didn't want to leave. I laid there beside him, his eyes still closed, and I thought about the day we met. A summertime party at a mutual friend's house. I was sitting alone when he came and sat beside me.

There were small flirts and plastic cups filled with sangria. We chatted about movies and our favorite Mexican restaurants around town. He pushed his hair out of his face, and I swooned for him. At the end of the day I went straight home and wrote everything down.

When we finally pulled ourselves out of his bed, he offered me a cup of coffee. While he poured the hot water over the freshly grounded coffee beans, I sat on the couch and wondered what he was thinking. What was going on underneath all that messy, curly hair?

He sat beside me, and we sipped our plain coffees from mismatched mugs. We took turns playing songs on our phones and explaining why they mattered to us. Why a certain lyric or sound stuck with us throughout the years.

I was happy when I met him. Blindly content with my life, not realizing that I was missing something all along. And now that I had found it, I didn't want to ever lose it.

A pool day. Just me and him and a few of our close friends. We sat by the shallow end with IPAs in hand laughing and chatting about our long, busy work weeks.

My feet dipped into the cool oasis, while he stood in the waist-deep water beside me, his hand on my leg.
"We should go to the arcade bar up the road later today, would you wanna do that?" he asked. I was at a point where I couldn't believe he wanted to spend any more time with me.

This was the sixth day in a row.

"I love that bar," I said. "But we've all been drinking...how will we get there?" He pulled himself up and out of the pool to sit beside me. His soaked shorts leaked onto the pavement and underneath me.

"I can drive us. I haven't had that much to drink today."

"Are you sure?" I asked my eyes squinty.

"Yeah of course, don't you trust me?" He asked with a smile, "How is this relationship going to work if you don't trust me?"

"I do," I said. "I do trust you."

As we drove down the highway towards the bar it started to rain. A full-on storm with flashing lights and loud booms. The small moments of silence when we passed under highway bridges and the rain was silent soothed me and made me sleepy.

Without a thought, I reached my hand over and placed it on his thigh. Quickly, he placed his hand on top of mine. I felt happy. I felt safe.

At the arcade, we stood on opposite sides of a table with a Pac-Man game built into it. I won the first round but then lost the next five because I couldn't keep my eyes off of him. The game didn't matter, I was just happy to be in his presence. To be standing across from him. His focus was like none other, and I admired his ability to be so still when my entire world had fallen into a shaky excitement.

After a few more games of Pac-Man, we moved onto a pinball machine. He stood behind me and watched as I tried and failed multiple times to beat the high score. Every time the ball slipped through the cracks and I lost, he laughed and put more quarters in.

"Go again!" He yelled, "You're going to beat it or we will never leave, I swear!"

"We might be here all night then," I retorted with a laugh.

"Ahhhh, maybe we should just go home then," he said as he took my hands from the machine.

My head was dizzy from all the beers I consumed throughout the day and my eyes were tired from all the sun. I turned towards him and rested my head on him. The music in the bar vibrated in his chest as if it were hollow.

Our daily routine fell quickly into place. Coffee in the morning in the mismatched mugs and movies at night with a beer or a bottle of wine. We took turns picking out shows and movies on Netflix or playing songs from YouTube. Long chats about our family traditions for different holidays and cuddles on the couch while a random Netflix show played. And even though it was summertime in the city and the heat radiated from his brick building, he held onto my body tight as if he wanted it forever.

One night he held my hand while the credits of some corny scary movie scrolled. My eyes were heavy but I did not want to sleep. I wanted to feel alive with him all night under the covers, and we did.

I laid beside him out of breath, wide smile, his hand still in mine. I couldn't help but blush when he leaned over and kissed me on the cheek. A gesture that, to me, meant that this wasn't just a hookup. That feelings were developing beyond pool days and wild nights out at the bar.

"Thank you," I said and he smiled.

"Did you just thank you me for sex?"

"I did," I said laughing.

He turned over onto his side and pulled me close to him. His hand interlocked into mine. A kiss on the lips and one on my forehead, and quickly we both fell asleep.

In the middle of the night, I felt a hand on my back. I opened my tired eyes to find that I had rolled to the other side of the bed away from him, and his hand was searching in the dark to pull me back.

I laid still to find out what he would do. His hand grazed my back until it found my shoulder and slid down my arm to grab my hand. Two soft yanks that begged, *please hold onto me.*

I rolled and pulled him close and placed a kiss on his cheek. His body fit perfectly up against mine. All of the bends in our bodies from neck to hips to knees, we fit like the last piece of a puzzle.

I woke the next morning with a smile. I felt braver than I had in years. Like I had been doing the same motions for all this time and all at once, I changed. But it wasn't unilateral. More like I had changed with him. Side by side we grew into something new and lovely, and I never saw it coming. *When I hear happy songs I think of him, and when I hear sad songs I think of no one, because the guys who they were once attached to no longer matter.*

I found myself in this treacherous place between wanting to spend all of my time with him and not wanting to be too much. Stuck between whether or not just because he asked me to come over every night, if I should. Was I giving him too much, too soon? I didn't care if I was. I was making up for lost time.

I mean, why would he invite me, if he didn't want me around? Why would he hold my hand, if he didn't care? And why would he kiss me hello and goodbye, if he didn't miss me when I was gone?

I laid in my bed alone. The morning sun shined on my face to tell me it was time for me to get up and make a cup of coffee.

Sunday mornings were my favorite. I sat on my front porch with my hand-made mug of coffee and a book about two complete opposites finding each other and falling in love.

I sat and thought about whether or not I thought I was falling in love. Something I didn't think I had ever experienced. I would just know, wouldn't I? Like in the books and movies, they just *know*.

My lovey thoughts were interrupted by my phones loud chime. I reached over and unlocked my phone to a "wanna get breakfast?" text.

"Of course," I typed out and hit send.

"On my way to scoop ya up!" He responded.

Maybe I was falling in love. Maybe I was simply infatuated. Honestly, it had only been a month since we met. I'm not sure if I believed it could happen that quickly.

We sat at a table on a balcony of this brunch spot he knew. Clinking glasses filled with mimosas, blueberry pancakes, and an assortment of donuts. We stuffed our faces and when the bill came we split it in half.

On the car ride home, he held my hand. Never had I met someone with whom I was so comfortable. My anxious tendencies didn't bother him. He soothed them. Kept me still when I wanted to shake. Kept me sitting when I wanted to pace.

Instead of dropping me off at my place, he brought me to his, where we took a long and much-needed nap. As my eyes drifted shut with his hand in mine I thought, this is truly and treacherously *something*.

Forget what I said. I am definitely falling in love.

It didn't matter that he needed some time to himself, because I think I did too. But by day four without his hands or his lips or his sunny laugh, I found I missed him. Like I had never in my life for anyone, I wanted him beside me again.

A deep anxiety sank slowly through my body. Do I text him? Call him? Is it being too much to want him near me again? After five years of being content on my own, I didn't know if it was okay to want someone like this after only a month. Were there rules? And if there were, how far could I bend them before they broke?

I paced around my apartment as I sipped my lonely cup of coffee. I didn't want to feel this type of emotional. It went against everything that I wanted and created for myself. I had never needed a man in my life, but maybe I did need this one.

I stopped myself. Forced myself into a chair to calm down. Told myself that this was just an infatuation. That it was normal to be this way, especially after being alone for so long.

I was drowning. My body swirling out of control. My hands desperately pulling myself upwards and out. My lungs gasping and begging for air.

My phone chimed, and when his name showed up on the screen it was like he reached in and pulled me out. And then when I read the "I think we need to talk" text, it was like he shoved me back under. *I want to say that it's his loss, but I think it might be mine.*

I laid in my twin-sized bed, unable to move. Staring at the blank white ceiling. How could I let this happen?

Our talk was replaying over and over again in my head. His words so direct and matter of fact. As if he had either planned them in advance or just knew so badly how much he meant them.

The night before I sat there on his couch and absorbed every word, a new wound with each syllable. My hands were tied.

"This isn't an end," he assured me. "I love you and I love our friendship. I just can't have anything more than that right now."

"I understand," I said even though I didn't. Did I make this whole thing up in my head? Did I create something that simply wasn't there? I had always been so careful.

I made myself a cup of coffee and sat on the carpeted floor of my small studio apartment. Deep breath in, deep breath out. My sweater smelled like him. Woodsy and musky. It was like he was beside me and my head was resting on his shoulder. I let myself believe it.

A week passed without him, but on a Tuesday evening, I found myself back in his arms. Lying on his couch propped up with his head on my chest, as he dozed. I had gone over to his place because he wanted to talk, but instead, we decided to put a movie on.

"Can we just live in ignorance tonight?" He asked. "I just want to cuddle and feel you and be happy. I don't want complicated."

Of course, I couldn't resist the offer. I wanted it to be simple too. I wanted to love him and for him to love me back. I could have lived in that suggested ignorance forever with him.

I woke up to him giving me a small shake, "Hey, the movie is over. Let's go to bed."

"Hmm?" I murmured. "Yeah, okay."

He held my hand and led me up the steep staircase to his loft bedroom. I pulled off my jean shorts and fell into the bed beside him. He pulled me in and kissed me on the cheek, and then again on my lips.

He was all that I wanted, and he knew it, but it didn't matter. Half of me wanted to go back to the person that I was before I met him. Light and airy and carefree. Not a worry in the world. Another half wanted me to hold on forever and not let go. Keep all of the wild nights and the spectrum of emotions that came with them. But to hold on, I would need his help.

The next morning we were back on our routine. I sat on the couch finding a playlist for the background while he poured hot water over freshly ground coffee beans.

He came and sat next to me on the couch while the coffee rinsed through. His hand rested on my leg while he scrolled through his social media. Why couldn't it always be this simple?

"Are we going to talk?" I asked shyly. I didn't want to disrupt him but I also had so much to say. So much to work through. Because how could he say he doesn't want me, but continue to have me.

"Do you feel like we need too?" he asked and I nodded. He stood and grabbed the finished cups of coffee from the counter. "Okay, let's talk then. I want you to always feel comfortable telling me what's going on."

I poured myself out in front of him and he picked up every word and studied them intently. He held onto every word carefully and delicately as to not miss a single one. He heard me.

Another three nights passed that I didn't hear from him. After our talk, I had, in a way, expected it. But it still hurt just as bad. There is truly nothing like it when your brain is sad and your stomach is twisted.

It was time for me to start rebuilding all of the dark blue walls that I let him tear down. Or should I? I considered the possibilities of this experience. What had this cruel summertime fling taken away from me? But what did it give me?

Even if I couldn't pinpoint them quite yet, I knew there were lessons learned here. Hard lessons that were necessary. Maybe this heartbreak was just a step finding the real thing for me. No matter what that thing may be.

I sat in a coffee shop on the street between his and mine. A coffee shop I passed multiple times on my way to his place which was only three blocks from mine. Coffee in hand, I just wanted to be close to him. Hoping he might walk by and join me and hold my hand and tell me I was all he wanted.

On my way home I stopped at the store and bought a bouquet of daisies and a vase. Something nice to look at for my nightstand. The first thing to see when I wake up in the morning and the last thing I see before I sleep.

We sat across a table from each other. He wanted to get breakfast but he hadn't told me why. I mean we hadn't talked in almost four days. But still, I responded with a "yes" within seconds. I felt weak.

We ordered our food and the server filled the white mugs with steaming coffee. "So how have you been?" he asked me casually.

I blew on the surface of my black coffee and took a short sip. How honest could I be with him? I still wasn't sure what the rules for this were. "I am good," I said. "I actually went on a date last night." His eyes met mine as he finished his long sip.

"Oh really? That's great!" he said. "How did it go?" My throat was dry, my cheeks were warm. I shouldn't have said anything, but now I had no choice.

"It went well..." I said nervously. "I, um, it was good. He's sweet and handsome and he knows...exactly what he wants, and that feels nice."

His face wasn't happy or sad or excited, just flat. "But you know, it really just made me realize...it made me realize that." I struggled to make the words come out. "I realized that I don't want to date anybody else but you. I don't want to do this with anyone else."

His eyes were sympathetic. This wasn't a surprise to him. My feelings for him were clear from day one, and the fact that he didn't want me the way that I wanted him wasn't his fault. Or mine for that matter. The server stopped to top off our drinks. The clinking glasses and small chat filled the empty silent space between us.

"And I know that's not what you want," I continued. "But I have to be honest with you because it's not fair for either of us, if I'm not honest. If we aren't honest." He nodded in agreement, took another sip of his coffee and I could see in his eyes he was thinking of exactly how to respond.

"I'm happy you told me that," he said. "And I care about you a lot. You know that. You know that I do...and maybe I need to say that to you more often. But I can't give you what you want. You want a relationship. You want a boyfriend, and I can't give that to you right now."

I don't know why I said anything. This was the response I knew I would get. The server placed our plates full of food on the table.

"Enjoy!" She demanded of us, but how could I? He smiled and nodded at her and refocused on me.

"Listen," he said. "I want you to keep your options open. We can keep doing what we are doing, and if you go on a date, well, that's great. And if you date someone enough that we have to stop this, then that's okay."

It was a concept that I didn't understand. What did that make us? Friends with benefits? It was confusing. Because it's not like he would just call me to go out and then have sex and send me home. We cuddled, and he'd hold my hand through the night. And make us coffee in the morning and kiss me goodbye when I had to leave for work. By textbook definition, we were a couple.

"I can be okay with that," I lied. "We can do that."

I sat beside him in the park. There was an outdoor concert in the city. Neither of us had heard of the cover band but we thought it sounded like a fun idea anyway. Crowds of people, all ages and types, sat on blankets in the grass around us.

It had been three weeks since that morning at the breakfast place. Our routine hadn't changed, and truly, I did feel okay with it. I was having fun. For the first time in a long time, I was feeling something, and even though sometimes it was bad and other times it was good, it was at least *something*. My life had been a static line, and now it was crooked and exhilarating.

The late afternoon was still bright and hot. A line of sweat traced my forehead as we waited for the small band to set up and the sun to go down. A bottle of cold rosé the only thing to help us battle the heat.

"How was your day today?" he asked me.

"I didn't do much. Got some work done. Wrote a good chunk of what I have due this week." We didn't talk about my work as a writer often, mostly because I was shy about it. Also, because I wasn't ready to tell him that a lot of what I was currently writing was about him.

"How is the book coming anyway?" He placed his hand on my knee and even though it was sweaty, I didn't mind.

"It's going well," I said. "Just a few more chapters and it'll be finished. I feel really worried about it though. Like it will never truly be what my publisher wants it to be."

"It's going to be so good." He said elongating each vowel individually. "Oh look the band is starting!"

We swayed to the songs we didn't know and hummed to the melodies that we did. There was a couple in front of us. Holding hands and smiling, their noses almost touching, swaying to the smooth beat sounds of the band.

I caught myself staring at them as they laughed and danced and kissed and when the one with blonde hair dipped the one with red hair I almost lost it. I thought to myself, why was it so easy for some and so hard for others. If I cared for him and he cared or me, why couldn't we just *be*. Why did we continue to play this game of cat and mouse?

Even though it had only been four months since I met him and even though it scared me to my core I knew what I wanted. I wanted him. I wanted him more than I could write into words in the stories that I wrote into my books.

Looking his way, I admired his focus on the music. The way he bopped his head to the drums and how his eyes were so focused it was like I wasn't even sitting beside him. And seriously I almost said it right then. Spilled out every love song and poem into the air to show him how I felt. But would that be enough? I stopped myself. I had to play it cool. I couldn't do it. I couldn't ruin this perfect ignorant place we inhabited.

The band closed out with a banger of a song and we picked up our mess on the grass. Three empty wine bottles, a blanket that was made for me by my aunt, a few empty snack containers. We loaded them into my bag and he said to me, "We better hurry and get to the car before we get stuck in the traffic."

He grabbed my hand and started to pull me through the crowd of tipsy concert goers. His thumb massaging the palm of my hand as we walked and maneuvered through the throng. A flame of excitement was building up inside of me. I couldn't hold it in any longer.

I stopped him from moving forward. People pushed passed all around us. He looked back at me still gripping my hand, "Come on we have to get to the car."

"I...I ca-" I stuttered. There was a light breeze and the sun was setting behind him so I could barely make out his cerulean eyes. I was suspended in the moment.

"What's wrong? Are you okay?" He took a step back towards me and came into focus. I knew what I needed to do. I knew what I needed to say.

"I love you," I said quietly, softly enough that maybe he couldn't even hear me. "I do, I do I love you so much. And I know that is the last thing you could ever want to hear from me and I have just been holding it in and against me for so long," I was losing my air. "And I know I said that I would be okay with being just friends who do whatever it is that we are doing but I'm not. I'm really just not okay with it at all. I lied because something felt better or easier or I don't know what but something felt better than nothing."

I could see him taking in every word I was throwing out to him. Hoping he would catch one and hold onto it. Hoping he would hold onto me. His eyes like glass and his curls blowing lightly in the wind. "And you don't have to say anything back if you don't have the words but if you do I can take it I promise I can take it. I'm wide open here. But I can't keep it in any longer. I love you. I love you so much every minute of every single day and I hope that somewhere in you...somewhere even if it's deep down or if it's hard to find...or even if it takes you time...I hope you can love me too." I released every ounce of air I had left in my lungs for him.

The space between us was still and silent. People moved passed in slow motion. Sounds of crowds muffled by the words I had just filled the air with. And finally, he opened his mouth to speak.

CPSIA information can be obtained
at www.ICGtesting.com
Printed in the USA
LVHW112338111119
637079LV00007B/150/P